"Your lover is waiting for you!"

Lewis snapped the words out like bullets. "If you perform well he'll probably get you another film part— just the way he got you this one!"

Her face very white, Lori said desperately, "Lewis, please—I can explain. Nicholas Hayman isn't my lover, he's my—"

But he interrupted her harshly. "My God, and to think I fell for that act of wide-eyed innocence! Was I just another helpful contact you could use to get into more films? Is that all I meant to you? And did you really think I was so besotted that I'd turn a blind eye to your other lovers?"

Numb with hurt and despair, Lori stared at the man she loved. Couldn't he see that her passion was for him and him alone?

Other titles by

SALLY WENTWORTH
IN HARLEQUIN ROMANCES

Other titles by

SALLY WENTWORTH
IN HARLEQUIN PRESENTS

CHAPTER ONE

'Miss West?'

Lori turned with a sigh of relief at the sound of her name and found a bespectacled young man dressed casually in faded jeans and a tee-shirt looking at her expectantly. The tee-shirt had *The Siege* emblazoned on it in large red letters, proclaiming to everyone at the airport that he was a member of the film crew. She smiled. 'Yes, I'm Lori West.'

He merely nodded, not returning the smile, and bent to pick up her two largest cases.

'I've a company car outside. I'll put these cases in and come back for the rest.'

Lori watched him go with some surprise; her smile was warm and friendly, and being set as it was in a very lovely face there were very few people—especially men —who didn't immediately respond to it.

He was back within five minutes and picked up her other two cases—for which she'd had to pay excess baggage charges—while she gathered up her hand luggage and followed him out of the comparative coolness of the airport building into the May sunshine. It had been cold and wet when she'd left Gatwick, but here in Rhodes the temperature was already in the eighties and the sky was a deep, clear blue without a cloud in sight.

'Mm, lovely,' she murmured, lifting her face to the sun. 'Is the weather always as good as this?'

The young man glanced up from stowing her cases in the trunk and said briefly. 'Yes. It stops raining in

April and doesn't start again until October.'

He went to open the back door for her, but Lori said quickly, 'Oh, I'd much rather sit in the front.'

When they were both seated, she tried again. 'But you haven't told me your name yet, or what your job is in the film crew?'

This was accompanied by another smile, but the young man seemed to be oblivious and answered rather abruptly. 'I'm Bill, and I'm only a production assistant.'

Lori began to suspect that he was shy and tried to put him at ease. She laughed slightly and said, 'Well, I was very glad to see you at the airport. I had to wait so long after the plane landed that I was beginning to be afraid that everyone had forgotten I was arriving today.'

Bill turned to her, and to her dismay she saw that his expression was now downright surly. 'It was only half an hour or so, and I had some things to deliver for the director first. You can't expect everything else to stop just because a replacement actress has finally turned up,' he added sarcastically.

Lori stared at him for a moment, completely taken aback by his rudeness. Anger started to mount and she began to retort, 'Now, look ...' but he was approaching a busy thoroughfare in the centre of the town and using his horn to clear the way so that her words were drowned beneath the noise. Slowly Lori sat back in her seat; although—like everyone else—she hated people to think badly of her, there seemed little point at the moment in explaining to this ill-mannered young man that he was entirely wrong about her. It was true that there had been a few days' delay between her acceptance of the completely unexpected offer to replace one of the stars in the film and her arrival in Rhodes, but

that was only because she had been in the middle of making a television play which she'd had to finish first. The producer of the film had tried to make her give it up and fly out immediately, but she had insisted on fulfilling her obligation, although she had been very much afraid that by doing so she might lose the film part altogether. Her luck held, however, and they agreed to wait until the play was finished, but even so it had been one mad rush to be ready to fly out here the minute filming was over; they hardly even gave her time to say goodbye to her mother before she was being whisked away to the airport with—she hoped—enough luggage to last her through the three months it would take to produce *The Siege*.

A look of excitement came into her eyes as she thought about the film. She still couldn't quite believe her luck. The female lead, an international actress, had backed out of the part after only two weeks' shooting, the reason being kept a close secret, and the whole of the showbiz world was agog to see who would be chosen to take her place. Lori hadn't dreamt in a million years that she would even be thought of for the part, so she had been astounded when the producer had flown to England especially to offer it to her. At first she had been slightly suspicious that her godfather, who had interests in the film world, might have had a hand in her selection, but the producer was the head of his own independent film company and had explained that they wanted someone who resembled the original star so that they could use several long shots that had already been filmed. Production costs being what they were, Lori could well believe it.

It was only after she had accepted the part that doubts began to hit her; although she was an experienced stage actress and had been in numerous television plays, she had never before taken part in a film, let alone the full-scale epic that *The Siege* was rumoured to be. She had looked up old trade magazines to find out what she could about it and was dismayed to read that the cast included a big male Hollywood star who was playing a character role, and also a sought-after young American actor—who had made his name in a glossy television serial and been nominated for an Emmy award—as the male romantic lead. And if that hadn't been enough to unnerve her, finding out that the director was no less than Lewis Brent, who had a reputation for pushing his actors to the extremes of their talent and being a hard taskmaster, had certainly done so. But all his previous films had been superb; Lori had seen them all and every one had been the kind of experience that burned into the mind and seared the emotions. Unforgettable. Exhilarating. Whether they were pure escapism or set out to raise question-marks in the mind, they had all been brilliantly executed and brought fame to many hitherto unknown actors. And to her? Lori was afraid to even begin to hope for such a miracle; she could only pray that her work would be acceptable and she wouldn't let anyone down by her inexperience.

She glanced again at her companion, but he was purposely over-intent on his driving, determined not to look in her direction. Lori sighed inwardly; his churlish behaviour and the wait of nearly an hour at the airport were hardly an auspicious beginning to her new job and could only add to her lack of confidence, but she determinedly shrugged it off; perhaps he had personal problems of his own. But she would have given a lot to be able to ask him all the questions that were bubbling over in her mind: what was the plot of the film, how far had shooting gone, why had her predecessor left, what were the crew like—these, and a host of others, were longing to be answered. And most of all she would have liked an answer to the question she wouldn't have dared to ask in any circumstances—what was the great Lewis Brent really like to work with? But it seemed that she would just have to wait until she found someone more amiable to ask or until she found out for herself the hard way.

Instead she looked out of the window and was soon lost in the pure enjoyment of this beautiful Greek island. Everywhere there were flowers; great hanging hedges of purple bougainvillaea and bushes of pink oleander in the gardens of the square, white-washed houses, and the brilliant red of hibiscus growing wild at the side of the road that bordered the sea. A sea that was quite different from her expectations; she had thought it would be the deep, calm blue of the Mediterranean, but this sea was almost grey with a strong tide that sent quite high waves pounding against a shore of shaley, dull-coloured sand.

Bill continued to follow the coast road further and then turned off and pulled up in front of a large modern hotel encircled by green lawns and hedges and more banks of flowers. Lori climbed thankfully out of the car; it had been a long, tiring journey and she longed to shower and change her clothes. A porter came to help with her luggage and Bill paused to speak to the receptionist and was handed a key. He went off again without a word, obviously expecting Lori to follow him, which she did in growing resentment at his boorish attitude. She said nothing, though, in the elevator because the porter was with them, but she deter-

mined to have it out with Bill as soon as they were alone
again. At the seventh floor he led the way to room
number 712 and opened the door for her to go in.

They brought in her bags and, still simmering with
annoyance, Lori turned to Bill, but the porter was
looking expectantly at her and as Bill made no move
to do so, Lori groped in her bag for a tip. And then she
heard Bill say, 'So long,' and before she could stop him
he had gone. Quickly she pushed some money into the
porter's outstretched hand and ran after him, but the
elevator doors were already closing before she reached
them.

'Well, really!' Lori stood with her hands on her hips
and glared at the doors indignantly. Of all the nerve!
He hadn't even told her when she could expect to be
asked to start work, whom she should contact, or anything.

Then she realised that she had left the door of her
room wide open and hurried back to it. The room was
fairly large, a double with two single beds against the
right-hand wall. There was also a small bathroom just
to the right of the door that was lit by a fluorescent
light. Lori looked at herself in the mirror and grimaced.
The pressure of the last few days and the long journey
hadn't done her any good at all, she looked positively
haggard. But this was an overstatement, the face that
looked back at her was still lovely; heart-shaped, with
high cheekbones and a straight nose between long-
lashed eyes as green and sparkling as emeralds in the
sunlight. Her hair, a deep gold with a hint of red,
framed a face that would have been perfect if it hadn't
been for the slightly determined and obstinate set of her
chin.

Coming back into the main room, Lori crossed to the
French windows and opened the door on to the bal-

cony. A surge of disappointment hit her as she saw that the room was at the back of the hotel and looked out, not over the sea as she had hoped, but over the rather untidy concreted yard of the hotel and an area enclosing tennis courts. Beyond them a hill covered in rather scrubby-looking bushes rose quite steeply, bisected along its width by a narrow road. Soon she turned back into the room, her feeling of disappointment growing. She knew that the cast and crew of a film had to pay for their own accommodation while on location and that it usually worked out cheaper if the company took over part or the whole of a hotel, but she had certainly expected something more pleasant than this. But she had no right to complain; she was only a very new, very inexperienced Johnny-come-lately, and all the rooms on the lower floors with sea views were bound to have been snapped up when the crew first arrived, so she would just have to make the best of it. But she couldn't help wondering just what accommodation an international star like her predecessor had been offered and what had happened to it when she left.

She started to unpack, but the thought of a shower was still uppermost in her mind, and after a while she remembered catching a glimpse of a swimming-pool as they had arrived at the hotel. The sun beckoned with irresistible fingers and she impulsively decided to go for a swim before she finished unpacking. Quickly she opened another case and pulled out a yellow bikini that had slits up both sides of the bottom half, joined by thin laces. It took only two minutes to change and put a long, kaftan-style robe over her costume, but before she left the room she hesitated. Perhaps she had better check with the reception desk first in case there were any messages for her. But the operator assured her that there weren't, so she picked up her bathing cap and took the elevator down to the ground floor. For a moment she stood undecided, wondering which way to go, but then she saw several people in beach clothes going down some wide marble steps and followed them to glass doors leading out to the gardens and the pool.

There were lots of loungers set around the edges of the pool and Lori dropped her robe on to one while she pushed her hair under the cap. Her long-legged, slim figure attracted a great many glances from the other guests, the men's openly appraising, many of the women frankly envious, but Lori ignored them; it was something she had got so used to over the years—especially since becoming an actress—that she had become thick-skinned and was now almost oblivious to it.

The water in the pool struck cold at first and she gasped and shivered, but then turned and swam in a fairly competent crawl down the length of the pool to warm herself up. But after only a couple of lengths her muscles began to ache and she realised she was too tired for anything that energetic and rolled over to float on her back and rest for a while. Almost immediately a head appeared in the water beside her and a grinning young man who spoke to her in first German and then French tried to get to know her. Lori shrugged resignedly and headed for the side of the pool. She had also become fairly thick-skinned about men trying to pick her up and could deal firmly enough with them, making sure that she gave them no encouragement and letting them know in no uncertain terms that she wasn't interested. This worked with all but the most persistent cases, and it did now as she simply turned her back on the young man and walked away, but sometimes the men wouldn't take no for an answer and this had led to rather nasty little scenes before she had got rid of them.

Her swim had left her skin tingling, but her muscles still ached. The lounger looked overwhelmingly comfortable and inviting; surely it wouldn't do any harm to rest for a minute and let her swimsuit dry off a little? She settled herself in the lounger and wondered why, when the film company had been in such an all-fired hurry to fly her out here, they hadn't bothered to contact her or give her any instructions on arrival. Perhaps they just liked to have everyone on hand ready to be called on when needed. She knew so little about filming, but had got the impression from talking to other actors that compared to stage and televison work it was usually organised chaos with everyone at the mercy of the vagaries of the weather. Although the weather in Rhodes must surely be ideal, Lori thought dreamily as she gazed up at the pure blue of the sky. It was so hot; she could feel it soaking deep into her skin, drying her swimsuit and warming her like a softly enveloping duvet. Her eyes closed and within seconds she was asleep.

A shadow falling across her face woke her and she moved lazily, still half asleep and reluctant to surface.

'Lori! Lori, wake up!'

She blinked and lifted a hand to shade her eyes from the sun. Then she gave a little gasp of surprise and sat up, fully awake now. 'Why, Tony! What on earth are you doing here?'

The young man reached down a hand and pulled her to her feet. 'The same as you—I've got a part in *The Siege*.'

'Oh.' Lori received this piece of news with some misgivings. She had first met Tony Rodgers eighteen months ago when they were both doing a winter season with a Shakespeare company in the Midlands, and they had dated steadily for a few weeks, but then Tony had wanted to take the relationship further and had asked her to live with him, getting really nasty when she had steadfastly refused. This wouldn't have mattered so much if he hadn't brought his frustration and resentment at her rejection into the theatre with him, creating a strained, tense atmosphere that had affected his performance. As a result he had been asked to leave. That night he had got very drunk and after the show had tried to force himself on her, then shouted abuse, and blamed her for what had happened when she'd screamed and some of the cast had pulled him off her.

So she looked at him now uncertainly. He was extremely good-looking, tall and slim, his face as handsome as a Greek god's under his well-cut fair hair. Too handsome for his own good really; he had come to expect every woman he wanted to jump into bed with him whenever he crooked a finger, and he just hadn't been able to accept the fact that Lori wouldn't do the same.

He regarded her now with one eyebrow slightly raised, his eyes running over her in sardonic appraisal before he said with a slight trace of irony in his voice, 'Quite a coincidence, isn't it?'

Lori picked up her towel and began to pat herself dry. 'Not really. As we're both in the same profession we were bound to run into each other again some time. Have you been busy?' she added rather stiltedly, still thrown by his unexpected appearance.

He gave a somewhat wry grin 'Oh, I've managed to keep the wolf from the door, although things got pretty tight after you got me thrown out of the Shakespeare season.'

Lori straightened up. 'Let's get this straight, Tony. You got yourself thrown out. You let your personal feelings affect your work, and it was your unprofessionalism that lost you the job, not me,' she retorted sharply.

For a moment his eyes appeared to Lori to be full of something approaching hatred, but it was quickly gone as he gave her one of his most charming smiles. 'Ah well, that's all water under the bridge now. And I'm very glad to see you here; I don't know anyone else in the cast and it will be good to have someone from the theatre world to talk shop with.' His smile became warmer, sensual. 'And you haven't changed a bit. Still as lovely as ever. Although perhaps you've filled out just a little in the right places,' he added, letting his eyes run slowly over her, stripping her.

Lori stepped back as from a physical touch. Her voice cold, she said shortly, 'You're right, I haven't changed —*in any way*,' she emphasised.

Tony's smile tightened, but then he shrugged. 'All right, I get the message, but you can't blame a chap for trying. No hard feelings, okay?'

She looked at him searchingly for a moment, wondering if she could trust him, but he seemed genuine enough and she was more than willing to meet him halfway; she was sure that she was going to need a kindred spirit in this strange new environment, even if it was only to reminisce on earlier times with. And she would be grateful for any advice and guidance he could give her, of course, but at the same time she didn't want to create a situation where she would be in his debt in any way. She would just have to try and handle things very delicately. But she couldn't help giving an inner sigh of exasperation. Of all the people she knew in show business, the one who was working on the same film just had to be Tony Rodgers!

Lightly she said, 'Aren't you working today?'

'I was. But as there was a mad panic on to find you and no one else knew what you looked like, I was yanked off the set and told to scout round for you.'

Lori stared up at him in astonishment. 'What are you saying? Was someone looking for me? Why didn't you tell me straightaway?' Agitatedly she bent to pick up her kaftan and pull it on.

'I'm afraid meeting you again put it out of my head. When you didn't go to the production office as you'd been instructed or answer the phone in your room, Lewis started to hit the roof and sent people scurrying after you in all directions.'

'Lewis? You mean Lewis Brent, the director?'

'None other. And when Lewis Brent says run, then you run. Although,' he added with a slightly twisted grin, 'I suppose that when you walk into a starring role in the way you did, you can afford to ignore his instructions and turn up when you feel like it.'

As she slipped on her sandals Lori glared at him. 'Oh, don't be so ridiculous, Tony! You know that all that temperamental actress stuff just isn't my scene at all. I didn't receive any instructions, and I checked with the desk before I came out here that there weren't any messages for me. The lines must have got crossed somewhere. The man who drove me here from the airport was most unhelpful and he didn't tell me a thing.'

'Well, he probably didn't know anything—he's only a glorified messenger boy. But he reported that he'd delivered you to the hotel and then Lewis gave you an hour to settle in before he asked you to report to him. Then, when you didn't turn up, he gave you another hour's grace before he telephoned your room and started looking for you.'

Puzzled, Lori said, 'Two hours? But I've only been here for a ...' She stopped suddenly and reached out to look at Tony's watch, then groaned. 'Oh no! I was so tired that I fell asleep by the pool and must have gone out like a light. I thought I'd only dozed for a few minutes.' She groaned again. 'Oh hell! What a dismal way to start my first day. Still, it can't be helped now. I'll just have to get to the production office as fast as I can and apologise.' She started to hurry back towards the hotel buildings, Tony falling into step beside her. 'Where is the office?'

'It's here in the hotel. They took over one of the lounges and fixed it up as an office.'

Once inside, Lori walked quickly towards the elevators but Tony put a hand on her arm to stop her. 'You're going the wrong way, the office is down that corridor to the left.'

'But I have to go to my room and change first.'

Tony shook his head. 'The great man said I was to bring you straight there.'

'But I can't turn up like this,' Lori protested. 'I look a mess. I need to re-do my make-up and brush my hair and. . . .'

'Far better to turn up looking a mess than keep him waiting any longer,' Tony warned. 'That's unless you don't care how angry you make him,' he added sardonically.

Lori bit her lip. She had a feeling that she was going to need all the confidence she could get when she faced the director, but perhaps Tony was right; at least he would know that she came immediately she received his summons. 'All right, we'll go straight there.'

'Good.' Tony took her arm and hurried her down the corridor, and Lori approached the double door at the end feeling rather like a prisoner who was being led to the block.

As Tony held the door open for her and she stepped inside, it was almost like entering a different world. The room was cluttered with desks and people and there seemed to be half a dozen phones ringing at the same time. On one wall there was a huge-scale map of the island, looking rather like a war-map with coloured flags stuck in it to denote the various location sites the film crew would be using, and on the right-hand side of the room a projector and screen had been set up and several people were watching and discussing some rushes that were being shown.

But Tony gave her little time to look round before guiding her towards a large desk at the far end of the room. As they walked forward a gradual silence fell on the room as people caught sight of her and nudged one another, until Lori felt as if every eye in the place was on her. All, that was, except those of a tall, brown-haired man who was standing at the big desk with his back to them, examining some papers. He must have been aware of the sudden tension in the room, but he gave no sign of it, merely continuing with his task. It wasn't until they had walked right up to him and Tony had said, with more deference than he'd shown her earlier, 'Lewis, I've found your missing actress for you. She was sunbathing by the pool,' that the man finally turned round.

Afterwards, Lori could hardly remember what he looked like. All she was aware of then was his eyes. Grey eyes, the colour of new steel, they travelled slowly over her and grew cold.

He made no effort to speak to her and Tony added rather uncertainly, 'This is Lori West, Lewis.'

Lori knew that she ought to be abjectly apologising for keeping him waiting, but somehow no words would come; it was like the mental block that you sometimes get in the theatre when your lines suddenly dry up and you find yourself standing on a brilliantly lit stage knowing that hundreds of people are watching you and your limbs and voice are completely frozen.

The silence lengthened until Lori's nerves began to grate and she could feel her heart beating loudly in her ears.

At last the director said slowly, sardonically, 'Ah, yes, Miss West. How good of you to join us. I must apologise for inconveniencing you by taking you away from your sunbathing, but there are one or two small matters that require your presence if this film is ever to be made. Although we will, of course, try not to take up too much of your time.'

He had an attractive voice, low and level, and he spoke as well as an actor, but the vitriolic sarcasm in his tone made the colour drain from Lori's cheeks leaving her white-faced and trembling. And the fact that everyone in the room was openly listening to her humiliation at Lewis Brent's hands could only add to her misery.

He went on in the same tone, 'As you will have seen from your call sheet, the wardrobe department are waiting to take your measurements so that they can make any necessary alterations to....'

Lori found her voice at last even though it was shaking, 'C-call sheet?'

Tony interposed quickly, 'Lori hasn't been in a film

before, Lewis. She probably doesn't know what a call sheet is.'

'No one is more aware than I that Miss West is not a film actress,' the director answered derisively. 'A call sheet, Miss West, is the list of instructions given out by this office each evening to every member of the cast and crew telling them what filming is taking place the following day: where to meet, what scenes will be shot, what equipment and props will be necessary, that sort of thing. It also. . . .'

Two bright spots of colour had come into Lori's cheeks at his continuing derisiveness. 'I know what it is,' she told him, tight-lipped. 'I meant that I hadn't been given one.'

The grey eyes swept over her again, then he turned with exaggerated patience and looked at a girl who was seated at a much smaller desk nearby. 'Joan, did you see that Miss West got her call sheet, as I asked?'

The girl answered immediately, 'Yes, Lewis, I took it up to her room personally as soon as I'd booked the room with the management.'

Lori felt a wave of anger surge through her, bringing a flush to her cheeks. 'I tell you it wasn't there!'

For a moment his mouth curled contemptuously, then Lewis Brent gave a dismissive shrug. 'It hardly matters now anyway, it would be completely behind schedule and I don't intend to waste more time by arguing about it.' He looked round and beckoned a couple of women who had been hovering nearby over. 'Lydia, you'd better take Miss West's measurements while I tell her how far we've got with filming. This is Lydia Grey, our wardrobe mistress,' he added to Lori as an afterthought.

'What size shoes do you take?' the woman asked Lori.

'Oh—fours.'

She pursed her lips. 'Mm, you might be able to get into the ones we've had made, then. The previous actress had very dainty feet,' she added, making Lori feel like an elephant. 'You'll have to take off that kaftan, dear, I can't take your measurements with it on,' she said reasonably.

'But I. . . .' Lori stared at her appalled, feeling an irrational abhorrence of standing almost naked in front of this arrogant, dislikeable man. 'I've only got a bikini on underneath. Couldn't it wait until later?' she asked, lowering her voice.

The woman gave her a straight look. 'Not unless you want to antagonise the director even further.'

'Is anything the matter?' Lewis Brent broke in impatiently, as he waited, a sheaf of papers in his hand, to talk to her.

'No, nothing,' Lori answered rather hollowly, and undid the string at the neck of the robe and slipped it off her shoulders to let it fall at her feet.

People had started talking again for a few minutes, but now they fell silent once more and Lori could feel every eye running over her tall, slim figure as she stood in a shaft of sunlight from the window. Lewis Brent, too, looked at her. Lori had experienced many men's reactions on first seeing her in a swimsuit and most of them had been frankly sensual, but she had never before met anyone who seemed so completely unaware of her beauty and attractiveness. The eyes that came back to meet her rather defiant ones were entirely impersonal and cold. His voice was also icy as he looked round the silent room and said loudly, 'Doesn't anyone here have any work to do?' and there was an immediate bustle as everyone hastily got back to work.

As the women started to take her measurements he glanced at his papers, his voice authoritative as he got down to business. 'Now, as you know, we've already been on location for two weeks and have shot several scenes which included your part. I've been going through the rushes of these with other members of the crew and we find that there are about five scenes where the close-ups will have to be re-shot with your face, and we've decided to give priority to these. The wardrobe department will alter the necessary costumes tonight and we'll start filming first thing in the morning. Luckily all the sets are still in place for the indoor scenes.'

He paused while Lori lifted up her hair so that they could cut a lock to use as a sample for a wig, then went on, 'As you know from reading the shooting script, this is a period drama set in....'

Unhappily Lori broke in, 'I haven't got a script. I don't even know what the film is about.'

His lips thinned and he turned to his secretary again. 'Joan?'

'A shooting script was flown out to London as soon as we knew Miss West was going to be offered the part,' the girl answered readily.

'But I didn't receive it!' Lori protested.

'See that Miss West is given *another* shooting script immediately,' Lewis Brent instructed, his slight but deliberate emphasis of the word 'another' making it a downright insult.

Lori flushed hotly; she had taken just about as much as she could stand from Lewis Brent. 'I tell you I never received one!' Her voice rose. 'Are you accusing me of lying?'

Having already been told off once, everyone in the

room pretended to get on with their work while at the same time avidly trying to listen to the confrontation between the director and this completely unknown and untried actress. Most of them held their breath, astounded at her temerity and waiting for thunderbolts to descend on her head.

Lewis Brent became suddenly still and his eyes froze her, although she managed somehow to stare defiantly back at him. Then suddenly the fight went out of her and she muttered an apology, lifting a hand tiredly to her eyes.

He looked at her for a moment longer, then, much to her surprise, went on as if she had never defied him, had never capitulated. 'The film is basically the siege of Rhodes by the Sultan Suleiman in 1522 against the Knights of St John who had held the island for over two hundred years. Your part is that of a young girl whose ship is attacked by pirates, but she is saved by being disguised as a boy and manages to swim ashore on to Rhodes. There she's found by Sir Richard Gretton—that's the part played by Dean Farrow, the American actor, and the other romantic lead—and of course he mistakes you for a boy. As far as you're concerned the rest of the film is the development of a growing relationship between the two of you, which the knight tries to fight because he thinks it's an unnatural one. However, when he finds out who you really are he makes love to you, but then sends you away because of the vows of chastity he's taken when joining the Order of St. John. But then, while the island is besieged, you're captured by the Turks and he steals into their camp to rescue you. And in the end he takes you with him when the remaining knights are allowed to leave the island.'

Lori's eyes had lit with interest as he talked and she

felt a thrill of excitement and anticipation; the part was far larger and more important than she had been led to expect, and again she couldn't believe her luck.

But excitement was instantly quashed as Lewis Brent said repressively, 'Don't start getting any ideas about the film being a love story revolving round the two of you. The romantic angle has been written in simply as a sop to women picturegoers and because the production company insisted on it; it's purely incidental to the main story, which is about the six months' siege.' His eyes narrowed and he added, 'And if I think that your performance detracts from the film then the whole part will end up where it belongs—on the cutting room floor.'

The women had finished their measuring and Lori bent to pick up the kaftan and slip it on before she turned to face him, her eyes over-bright in her white face. 'Is there anything else you want to tell me?'

His tone became sarcastic again. 'Not at the moment. A call sheet for tomorrow's shooting will be sent up to your room, and if you could manage to arrive on time, preferably having learnt the dialogue for the scenes, we would all, of course, be extremely grateful. You can go now, Miss West—and I hope we haven't kept you from your sunbathing for too long. Joan, have you got the new script for Miss West?'

The secretary brought the fat shooting script and silently handed it to Lori, her eyes mocking.

'Thank you.' Lori took it and turned to look at the director, her face set. 'And thank *you*, Mr Brent, for your welcome to the company.' Then she turned on her heel and walked quickly from the room, head high, her eyes looking straight ahead and oblivious of the curious glances that followed her.

CHAPTER TWO

THE wait for an elevator seemed interminable, but at last one came and Lori was able to shut herself into the comparative sanctuary of her room. For a few minutes she leaned against the door, her eyes closed, willing herself to stop shaking. That man! That damnable man! Who the hell did he think he was—God? How dared he treat her so rudely—and in front of other members of the crew? Gradually her trembling eased a little and she moved slowly forward to sit on the edge of the bed and put a hand up to her mouth, biting hard to keep from crying.

Why? Why had he been so hateful? Okay, so she'd been late and there had been a mix-up over the call sheet and script, but surely that didn't warrant the way he'd treated her. His dislike of her seemed to have been already there, just waiting to be turned on her the moment she arrived, which was totally the wrong attitude for a man in his position. All right, he needed to be determined and authoritative when the occasion arose, but the basic criterion of a director was that he establish a good working relationship with his actors and put them at their ease so that he could draw the very best performance out of them. But instead he had deliberately antagonised her, and she knew that tomorrow morning when she started work she would not only be nervous because of her inexperience in this new genre, but would also be tense and on edge in case Lewis Brent started picking on her again, criticising her work in front of other members of the cast and carrying on this personal antipathy he seemed to have against her. And she had to work with him for three months!

The temptation to just turn round and take the first plane back to England, to run away from the whole sordid business, was almost irresistible. Lori actually got to her feet and started to put some things back into her case before she stopped suddenly and stood very still as a new thought came to her. Was that what he wanted? Was that what the whole nasty scene in the production office had been about? To make her feel so upset and unwanted that she would give up the part and go?

She began to pace up and down the room, trying to figure it out in her mind. Had Lewis Brent really tried to get rid of her? If he had, then the only reason she could think of was because he had wanted the part to go to someone else and had been overruled, which was unusual, because the director usually had an important voice when it came to choosing the cast; after all, he was the one who would have to work with them. And if he had had a disagreement with the producer over who should play her part, then it would suit Lewis Brent very well if she walked out or gave such a bad performance that he could justifiably say that she was no good and get her fired. And that thought made Lori wonder yet again why the original actress cast for the role had left. Was it because she had had the same treatment meted out to her?

Lori wasn't aware of having made a conscious decision, but she suddenly knew, quite certainly, that she wasn't going to let Lewis Brent push her out of the best chance she would ever have to establish herself at the peak of her profession. If she walked out now everyone in show business would get to hear of it and she'd be lucky if she ever worked again. In a profession where beautiful, talented girls are two a penny there was no room for anything but complete dedication to the art, and anyone who was too weak to stand the pace soon found themselves out of work or reduced to wearing G-string bikinis and draping themselves over hoods of cars at motor shows! And that was something Lori would never do. She had fought and worked to get where she was far too long to throw it all away just because a man like Lewis Brent had taken a dislike to her. It didn't matter what he handed out to her, she would take it on the chin and come back for more until this beastly film was finished. It was only three months, and three months wasn't very long. No? Only a quarter of a year, a whole summer! For a moment her heart failed her, but then Lori remembered the years at drama college and in repertory where her bit parts had gradually increased to the ingénue lead, and then the audition for a good part in the West End which had led to her break into television and roles that she could really get her teeth into. No, not for anything would she give all that up, not for the worst that Lewis Brent could hand out to her.

With this resolve firmly in mind Lori began to unpack, and as she emptied the last, smallest case and went to stow it away, she found the missing call sheet, completely hidden beneath it. Lori's face tightened; the typed sheet had been put on a small table-cum-desk in the corner of the room, and she remembered thinking that that was rather a strange place for the porter to have set down her case. But was it the porter? Perhaps it was Bill, who had picked her up from the airport and been so rude to her. Could it have been that he had done it deliberately, taking his cue—or even his instructions—from Lewis Brent? Slowly Lori picked up the sheet and read it through, but without really taking the text in. If she were right, then she had far more to face than she had first supposed. Had he turned everyone against her? If so, her position would be intolerable. She couldn't be on her guard against the whole film crew. Lori felt a cold, hollow feeling in her stomach and she had to sit down, her thoughts in turmoil. But she wouldn't just tamely give in, she wouldn't!

And somehow she overcame her fears and sternly told herself that she would feel better if she had something to eat, remembering that she had only had a snack meal on the plane all day. The call sheet had at least told her that she was entitled to dinner at the hotel and she decided to go down and eat at once and then spend the evening learning her lines for the next day's filming. A glance in the mirror did nothing to comfort her, though; her hair was dishevelled, her make-up nonexistent after her swim, and she was dismayed to see a red tinge to her skin where she had fallen asleep in the sun. No wonder Lewis Brent hadn't wanted her in his film. Oh well, at least that was one thing she could put right. If he saw her properly dressed and made up perhaps he wouldn't feel quite so antagonistic towards her.

But when Lori, looking sophisticated with her hair up and dressed in one of her prettiest dresses, made her way to the restaurant and was directed to a section set apart for the film crew, she saw that Lewis Brent wasn't among the diners and didn't know whether to be pleased or sorry. Tony wasn't there either and as the place was crowded she had to share a table with three other people who just stared coldly at her when she apologised for intruding on them, and then carried on their conversation, pointedly excluding her. Lori seethed, she had never in her life been treated so abominably and it was obvious that everyone was taking their cue from the director. She was hungry, but she found that the food choked her and after only a few mouthfuls she pushed her plate away, but forced herself to sit through the meal and not run out of the room as she longed to do. This was only a minor thing and she could take it. But for three months? The thought burned into her brain and seemed to stretch like an eternity, an eternity of being humiliated and ignored. When she left the restaurant at last Lori walked down to the beach and stood staring out at the sea for a long time. Then she squared her shoulders resolutely. Well, she would just have to show Lewis Brent and everyone else that she wasn't afraid. She would have to take each day as it came and then put it behind her. That way the time would soon pass and the longer she managed to last out then the nearer she would come to winning. They couldn't *keep* re-shooting scenes for new actresses. If she could just hold out for the first week or so then they would have to keep her, whether Lewis Brent liked it or not!

When she got back to her room she found that a new call sheet for the next day's shooting had been pushed under her door and she immediately sorted out the scenes in her shooting script and started to learn her lines. Years of training had given her a good memory and she didn't find it too difficult, but at exactly ten o'clock she was startled by the sound of what seemed to be a band tuning up right above her head, and within minutes her fears were fulfilled as a rock group with extremely loud, whining electronic instruments broke into the latest pop numbers. Going out on to the balcony, Lori looked up and saw that she was on the top floor of the hotel, but the roof was being used as an open-air night club and was crowded with people, many of whom were already dancing under the flashing, coloured disco lights.

Lori groaned and mentally cursed whoever had put her in this room; it must be the worst in the hotel! Picking up her script, she resignedly left the room and took an elevator down to the ground floor, looking for somewhere quiet to sit. There were several lounges in the hotel, but in one a television was on, in another a pianist was playing, and a third had a bar and she noticed among the people several groups of film workers, so that was out completely. She finally found the emptiness and quiet she sought in a card room where only two men were seated at a far table, absorbed in their game.

There were five scenes to be shot the next day, two of them very short, but in all of them she was to play opposite Dean Farrow, the young American actor, whom she hadn't yet met. She wondered what he would be like and—with a feeling of dread—whether he too would be as hateful towards her as Lewis Brent. She worked steadily on, making sure that she was word-perfect, knew her cues, and had carefully studied all the directions given for the scenes; she was going to make very sure that no one would be able to criticise her in this at least. It was nearly midnight before she rose tiredly to her feet to go back to her room. The men, too, had finished their game and left at the same time. One gallantly held the door open for her and said something in a language she didn't understand. She smiled and shook her head and the man, a jolly middle-aged, rather tubby person, tried out his broken English on her as they walked to the elevators while his companion went off to get his key from Reception.

Lori was still trying to understand what he was saying and nodding whenever she caught a word, when she suddenly had the prickly feeling that she was being watched. Quickly she turned and found herself looking straight at Lewis Brent who was waiting for an elevator at another block about twenty yards away. For a moment their glances held. The contempt in his eyes sent a flare of anger through her veins and Lori's chin came up as she glared back at him defiantly. But then his elevator came and he stepped inside as if she didn't exist.

Lori came slowly awake the next morning as the sunlight reached her. She stretched and went to turn over, but then was suddenly fully awake as she realised where she was. She sat up quickly and grabbed her bedside clock. Oh no! It was almost six o'clock. Quickly she leaped out of bed and ran to the bathroom. When she had got to her room last night she had closed the windows to the balcony to try to shut out the noise of the night-club, but this had also shut out the cooling breeze from the sea and the room had become stiflingly hot so that she couldn't sleep anyway. In the end she had opened the windows and stuffed cotton wool in her ears, which had helped to shut out the noise but had also made her not hear the alarm which she had set for five o'clock, giving her plenty of time to get to the first location by the required time of six-thirty.

Hurriedly she showered and dressed, not bothering with make-up—she would have to be made up on the set anyway. Breakfast too she would have to miss out on, although her stomach protested loudly. She threw her script and everything else she would need into a big clutch bag, adding a bottle of aspirins because her head was throbbing as much as the music above her had throbbed through into the early hours of the morning. Then she ran for the elevators, determined to ask at the reception desk for a change of room just as soon as she got back from filming that evening; she just couldn't take another night of that noise. Impatiently she tapped her foot as she waited for an elevator, but the lights showed that they were all stationary on the ground floor and in the end she found the service stairs and ran down them, arriving absolutely breathless at the bottom and worried sick that she would be late and give Lewis Brent an excuse to have another go at her.

But luckily she found a taxi outside the hotel, and when she gaspingly asked the driver to hurry he took her at her word and covered the two miles to Rhodes in record time, and she arrived on the set only a few minutes after six-thirty. And almost the first person she saw was the director. He glanced at his watch, raised one eyebrow, and said with icy politeness, 'Good morning, Miss West. They're waiting for you in Make-up, if you can spare the time, of course.'

All the scenes were to take place in various parts of the old city built by the Knights of St John and Lori would dearly have loved to look around her, but Lydia Grey, the wardrobe mistress, was on the look-out for her and grabbed her the moment she arrived.

'We've altered your first costume, but I want you to try it on before you go into make-up. This way.'

She led Lori to a nearby house, which the film company had evidently taken over, and up a flight of narrow stairs to one of the upper rooms. Here there were dozens of beautifully made costumes hanging on racks while several women were working away on electric sewing machines or by hand, busily preparing costumes for later scenes. Lori slipped out of her shirt and jeans and Lydia helped her to put on the long coloured tights and boy's tunic.

'Your hair will be hidden under a wig, of course,' the elder woman murmured as she looked Lori over critically, walking all round her. 'You're very slim, I know, and that tunic is cut very loose, but even so you still stick out too much for anyone to mistake you for a boy. You'll just have to wear a special bodice to hold you in. It will be hot, but it can't be helped.'

From the costume fitting Lori went straight to Make-up where the chief make-up man himself took her over and did several very clever things that took a lot of the femininity out of her face and made her look surprisingly boyish. And when the hairdresser added a raggedly cut wig that matched her own hair colouring the transformation was startling.

'It's got to be ragged,' he explained, 'because it was supposed to be cut very hastily in order to disguise you as a boy.' He, too, looked her over critically. 'Yes, I think you'll do.'

He led her out into a courtyard where the sun was now very hot even though it was still early morning. The place was an anthill of activity as everyone prepared for the first scene, the cinematographers getting their cameras into marked positions, the sound recorders setting up their equipment and microphones, extras being made up and positioned, the continuity girl checking that everyone looked the same as in the original shots, the set designers making sure that nothing later than the sixteenth century appeared in the scene. It was chaotic, bewildering and overpoweringly exciting. Lori stood and gazed for a moment and was instantly fascinated.

But she was given little time to stand and stare; she was led over to where Lewis Brent was standing in consultation with several other people, most of them in ordinary clothes, but one or two in costume. He kept her waiting for several minutes before he let himself become aware of her—then he turned and examined her as he would an animal he was thinking of buying.

'She's not dirty enough,' he said dictatorially, 'and she should still be a bit wet from the sea, not completely dry.'

So they took her away and wetted the wig and dampened down her clothes, then dirtied her up a little and presented her to Lewis Brent again, but still the director wasn't satisfied. 'She still doesn't look as if she's been washed up out of the sea. Take her down to the beach and roll her in the sand.'

When they brought her back for the third time with sand stuck in her hair, on her face and in her clothes he merely gave a small nod before walking away to talk to someone else. Lori didn't know what she was supposed to do, so she just stayed where she was, although in no time at all she seemed to get in everyone's way and kept having to jump aside or get knocked down as people pushed past her.

After about ten minutes Lewis Brent came back and with him he brought another actor dressed as a knight, a handsome, fair-haired young man whom Lori instantly recognised as Dean Farrow. If anything he was even better looking in the flesh than on film.

The director said offhandedly, 'Miss West, this is your co-star, Dean Farrow.'

Lori waited for a cool greeting, but instead the young

man grinned lazily, thrust out a hand and said, 'Hi. Welcome to *The Siege*.' And Lori was so surprised by his apparent friendliness that she could only stare at him and mutter inarticulately.

Lewis Brent looked at her sardonically. 'Lost your voice, Miss West? Let's hope you find it before we shoot the first scene.'

Lori would have given a lot to prove him wrong and voice the sharp retort that came to her lips, but he had beckoned over two more men whom he introduced as the production designer and the director of photography and then went on, 'We'd better have a skull session before we start so that....'

Despite herself, Lori's eyes widened and she blurted out, 'Skull session?'

He frowned exasperatedly, but Dean Farrow broke in with, 'That's film-makers' jargon for the talk the director has before a scene is played. It just means he tells everyone what he wants them to do.' He added with a grin, 'It had me fooled at first; I thought we were going to practise a fight where I got my head bashed in!'

Lewis Brent gave a wry grin. 'Bashing you on the head is about the only way I can get my directions into that thick skull of yours.'

Lori stared at him. Heavens, the man could actually make a joke! He had even come near the semblance of a smile. Maybe beneath that arctic exterior there lurked something faintly resembling a human being after all! But these thoughts were lost as he began to talk and she listened intently. His 'skull session' in reality turned out to be a lengthy briefing during which every aspect of the shots was worked out minutely with the cast and crew, and he illustrated his instructions by a diagram drawn on a blackboard showing where every key position of lights and cameras would be set up.

Part of his talk with the director of photography was technical and way above Lori's head, but during this time she had the leisure to study Lewis Brent more closely. She judged him to be only in his early thirties, but he seemed very self-assured, very energetic as he talked, with a strong, masterful face, tanned already from the Mediterranean sun. His hair was nut-brown and thick, and his left eyebrow was slightly higher than the other, giving him a quizzical and slightly arrogant appearance. His bone structure was good and he had a thin mouth that looked as if it might break into a smile at any moment. It was the sort of face that would have interested her if it hadn't been for his grey eyes that grew cold every time they settled on her.

The skull session over, they rehearsed the scene for positions and cameras a couple of times and then for dialogue and acting. Lori was fully expecting him to pull her up for the slightest error and was doubly glad that she had taken such pains to learn her part, although this scene wasn't very difficult. She had only to follow Dean as he walked through part of the old city, looking round her in wonder and fear and then trying to tell him who she really was, but being afraid to. As they went through the first acting rehearsal Lori was burningly aware of Lewis Brent's eyes following her every movement, every second waiting for him to call out some rebuke or criticism.

But it wasn't until they had gone right through the scene that he said sardonically, 'I know I told you to appear to be nervous, Miss West, but you don't need to look like a frightened rabbit that wants to disappear down a hole in the wall.'

Lori stiffened at his rebuke and was acutely aware of the grins it raised among several members of the crew. Tightly she replied, 'Thank you, Mr Brent, I'll bear that in mind.'

For a moment their glances locked and he said silkily, 'Then let's shoot it, shall we?' Then, loudly, 'All right, let's go.'

The clapper-boy hurried forward, there was a sudden complete silence all around her in which the sharp clap of the board sounded like a pistol shot, and Lori felt her throat go dry and her muscles tense with stage fright as she prepared to play her first scene in her first film. Of course it went wrong; it was bound to. As they walked down through the street Dean went a little slower than before, and Lori, looking round in awe as she had been instructed, bumped right into him and automatically said, 'Oh, sorry.'

'Cut!' The director's voice echoed through the old buildings. 'Let's take it again. And perhaps you could continue to also look where you're going this time, Miss West?'

Lori flushed and turned away to quickly walk back again, but Dean caught her arm and slowed her down. 'Hey, don't rush! It's getting pretty hot in this mediaeval tin can.' Then he grinned at her. 'Sorry, that was my fault back there.'

They shot the scene again and this time she forgot to look directly into one of the cameras. The third time she stood in Dean's shadow, and by the fourth time she was so uptight that she was shaking and mumbled her lines. She waited, miserably, for Lewis Brent's cutting tongue to flay her.

And this time his tone absolutely dripped with sarcasm. 'I'm fully aware, Miss West, that you regard this merely as a holiday, but there are others of us who are here to work, and strangely enough we do not have un-limited time to spend on one short—and I previously thought very simple—scene!'

Biting her lip in mortification, Lori walked with Dean back to the beginning of the set. It was very hot now and she could feel her skin starting to perspire beneath the heavy wig and the special bodice. A make-up girl came to dab away at her face and to wipe the perspiration that flowed freely off Dean's brow. Lori apologised to him guiltily; he must be burning hot inside the suit of armour and chain mail, even if it was made of lightweight modern material instead of the original metal.

He gave a good-natured grin. 'Think nothing of it. If I wasn't doing this they'd have me up on a horse fighting a battle—and that's really hot work!'

Lori gave a half smile and, emboldened by his sympathetic manner, asked hesitatingly, 'Is he always like this?'

'Lewis?' Dean gave a slight shrug. 'I guess he just got out of bed the wrong side this morning. He's usually a pretty good-humoured guy. Still, I guess making a film is a nerve-racking job when you've got the financial backers breathing down your neck, and especially when one of your stars quits and you have to re-shoot with an——' he broke off hurriedly.

'An unknown? Why be embarrassed to say it? It's perfectly true,' Lori said rather bitterly.

He shrugged. 'Even the biggest stars were unknowns once, Lori.' And he went off to get himself a drink of Coke from the ice-box.

Lori went to stand in the block of shade cast by an angle in the high wall and closed her eyes while she waited for the cameras to be got ready again. She put her hands flat against the wall, feeling the stone, hot and solid against her skin. They had stood for so long, these walls, had been built with such hope and purpose by men who had expected to carry on their way of life through countless generations. If she closed her eyes tight she could almost see them walking down the ancient streets in the rich panoply of their arms and tunics, almost hear the sound of swords clinking against armour. Slowly, Lori began to absorb the atmosphere of the past until it filled her mind. It was as if she pushed the present out of her brain and became the character she was to play. It was an ability—some would say a gift—she had, which lifted her out of the common sea of budding actresses and had gone a long way towards the successes she had had on the stage. It was something she found easier in the theatre because you naturally played a part from the beginning to the end, but with television it wasn't so easy because, like this film, scenes were so often shot out of sequence and it was hard sometimes to get the feel of the part. But now she concentrated, imprinting the character deep into her subconscious, and when the sharp noise of the clapperboard sounded for the next take, she wasn't nervous or afraid any longer. Lewis Brent didn't exist; no one existed except herself and Dean in the parts they were playing.

And this time it went perfectly from the moment they turned into the street until they reached the point where Dean, as Sir Richard Gretton, told her he was going to make her his servant and pointed towards his quarters. When Lewis Brent's voice called 'Cut!' it was almost like a magician snapping his fingers to bring her out of a trance. She jumped a little and blinked, again aware of everyone around her. With some trepidation she turned to look at the director, but he merely nodded to his assistant and said, 'Okay, let's get on to the next scene.' No words of praise, of course, for having got it right. But then, Lori thought wryly, she hadn't really expected any, had she?

In her next scene she was forewarned and was able to go and stand by herself for a few minutes just before the scene was shot and was again able to think herself into the part, and as it was in the same costume it didn't take very long, but the third scene necessitated a change of clothes and she was taken back to the house to be dressed in a page's outfit, to be re-made up and to have another wig fitted. It all took quite a time and when she finally emerged on the set she found that the lunch wagon had arrived in her absence. No one, of course, had thought to bring her a lunch-box and when she went over to it all they had left was lukewarm coffee in a plastic beaker and doughnuts.

When Lori looked round she saw that Dean was sitting with some other men and playing cards, so she took her coffee and doughnut and found herself a corner in the shade where she carefully hitched up the tunic of her costume and sat on the ground. She had a vague idea that the lead parts in a film were entitled to a chair with their name on it, but perhaps that was a myth, because there didn't seem to be any on this set. The crew and cast were predominantly male, with only her own and one or two very minor roles being filled by women. There were a few other women in the wardrobe and make-up departments and some secretaries and assistants in the production office, of course, but there were only the script girl and Lewis Brent's secretary who were permanently on the set. These two were now in animated conversation together and resolutely ignored her. Lori noted rather sourly that they had a couple of fold-up chairs and were tucking into the prepared lunch-boxes and a bottle of wine.

During the lunch hour a couple of taxis drove up to the set and several members of the crew who had been playing at another location joined them. Tony Rodgers was among them and he came straight over to her.

'You look like Little Jack Horner sitting in the corner,' he grinned.

Lori pulled a wry face. 'Well, I envy him his Christmas pie. It had to be better than this,' she said, indicating her scrap meal.

He squatted down beside her. 'How's it going?'

Answering with determined cheerfulness, she said 'Oh, fine. We've shot two scenes already. Aren't you working today?'

'Yes, we've been rehearsing a fight scene on the ramparts with the stunt co-ordinator, but we won't do the actual shooting until tonight. I think you're having some of your scenes there this afternoon, aren't you?' Lori nodded and he went on, 'How are you making out with Lewis?' He spoke lightly but was unable to keep the ardent curiosity out of his voice.

She shrugged. 'As you said, he's a hard taskmaster.' She would have liked to say a whole lot more, to unburden herself of the active dislike that was quickly growing into hatred of Lewis Brent, and if she had been sure of a sympathetic ear she probably would have done so, but although Tony was overtly friendly something made her hold back, to keep her feelings to herself.

'Driving you hard, is he?' Tony prompted.

'No more than I need, I suppose,' Lori countered, resisting his obvious wish for her to confide in him.

'And Dean Farrow? How do you get along with him?'

'Oh, he seems nice,' Lori answered readily, on safe ground here. 'I like working with him.'

Seeing that he wasn't going to get any more out of her, Tony started to talk about his favourite subject— himself, and told her about his part as one of the French knights. 'They kill me off half-way through the siege, but at least I get to die gloriously,' he added, exerting his charm to make her laugh.

After the lunch break he took himself off and everyone was driven up to the ramparts of the old fortifications where the rest of the scenes that day were to be shot. When Lori climbed up the steep steps to the top of the high walls the sheer size and immensity of them took her breath away. In the two hundred years in which the Knights of St John had owned Rhodes they had dug a huge dry moat with inner and outer fortifications of huge bastion walls with large round towers at intervals. And from where she stood she could see that the ancient walls formed an immense circle, bordered on one side by the sea where it guarded the two harbours of Le Port and Mandraki, the latter where the great bronze statue of the god Helios, the Colossus of Rhodes, was said to have straddled the entrance to the harbour in the third century B.C.

The filming that afternoon would have gone well as far as she was concerned if it hadn't been for little things that held up production and called Lewis Brent's wrath upon her head. Things started to go wrong when she put down a wine pitcher she was supposed to be taking to Dean and when she went to pick it up to shoot the scene she couldn't find it. Everyone had to look for it and it was finally found on the ground, half hidden by a shield. Naturally she got the blame for being careless, but Lori knew that someone had moved it on purpose to get her into trouble. Then a man, one of the small part players, deliberately tripped her during a crowd scene.

By this time Lori's nerves were beginning to fray, but a stubborn streak made her hold on to her temper and somehow carried her through to the end of filming, even though several more niggling little incidents occurred.

No one was more pleased than she when Lewis Brent called 'Cut!' for the last time and they were able to pack up for the night. She was left to take off her costume and remove her make-up alone, the members of those departments had gone long since, and when she emerged found the set deserted and quiet. She sat for a little while by herself, feeling exhausted and letting all the hurt that the day had brought ebb away, then she got a taxi back to the hotel and ate alone in the now almost empty restaurant. Afterwards she tried to change her room, but was told that the hotel was fully booked for the whole of the season and there wasn't anything else available. Resignedly she accepted this, too weary to care whether it was true or not, and went up to try and learn her lines for the next day's filming.

Somehow she got through the next two days, although by the end of each day's heavy schedule she felt like a zombie, what with intense concentration on her work and lack of sleep. Whether Lewis Brent was pleased with her work or not, she couldn't tell, for although he would say a word of praise to Dean or other actors, he never had one for her. But at least his sarcasm had diminished and he didn't seem to pick her up for every little thing as he had on the first day. Lori clutched thankfully at this thin straw, and was also grateful for the apparent friendship that Tony offered her. He was the only one to seek her out in between filming and she was so pleased to have someone to talk to that it never occurred to her to question his motives.

Often when they sat together Tony would put an arm negligently across her shoulders, and although Lori didn't particularly like it, she didn't obviously try to push him away; she knew that it was a habit of his to assume a proprietorial role whenever he was with a girl and she didn't think much about it. If the truth were told, she even welcomed it a little, especially when she saw Lewis Brent's cold grey eyes on them. At least he would know that she wasn't completely alone and friendless.

After filming on the third day she shared a taxi back to the hotel with Dean Farrow and was surprised when he asked her to go out for a drink at a local taverna after dinner. He seemed to enjoy the company of the other men in the cast and she had heard that he had the reputation of being a bit of a hell-raiser, often rolling up at the hotel in the early hours more than a little drunk.

She hesitated, but when he said, 'There's quite a few of us going along,' she shook her head determinedly. She was just too dog-tired to face an evening with people who had either ignored her completely or tried their best to upset her during the last three days.

But it was Saturday night and the noise from the night-club finally drove her out of her room and down on to the terrace of the hotel. There was no filming to-morrow, thank goodness, and so no lines to be learnt tonight, which was just as well because her head ached so much that she didn't think she'd be able to concentrate. A waiter came up to her and she ordered a drink of the local retsina, hoping it would help her to sleep. There was no one else from the film crew about; presumably they had all gone into town or to one of the many night-clubs in the area to live it up a little. Lori suddenly felt very alone again and almost wished she had accepted Dean's invitation; anything would have been better than this.

So she felt almost grateful when Tony Rodgers appeared on the terrace and immediately crossed over to her.

'So this is where you hide yourself away. I've been looking all over the hotel for you. I thought you might have gone out with Dean Farrow.'

'He asked me to,' Lori admitted, 'but I was too tired.' Then she added ruefully, 'I intended to have an early night, but my room is right under the night-club, unfortunately.'

'Oh, I see.' Tony dropped into the chair beside her. 'Well, if you can't sleep, how about coming for a stroll along the beach for a while? There's something I'd like to talk to you about.'

Lori looked at him rather suspiciously, but his manner seemed completely open and serious, and she couldn't help wondering and hoping that he was going to tell her why everyone in the crew was treating her so hatefully. If she knew why, then she could at least try to put things right. Making up her mind, she said quickly, 'All right, I'll come,' and hastily finished her drink.

There were steps down from the terrace that led to a broad, tree-lined walk leading to the road running parallel to sea which you had to cross to get to the beach. There were lamp-posts set at intervals along the walk, throwing pools of light that illumined the hibiscus flowers and turned them to a strange, drab colour. They passed several people as they strolled along because the walk was used as a short cut by hotel guests returning by taxi or bus from the town; they preferred to be dropped off at the main road and walk up through the gardens rather than have the taxi wait to drop them at the busy entrance to the hotel.

Tony seemed in no hurry and talked about Rhodes and the film as he ambled slowly along. Lori was impatient to hear what he had to say, but realised that he would probably try to get the most dramatic effect out of it and would keep her in suspense as long as he could. It was one of the things that had most put her off him before and he was unlikely to have changed, so she just had to content herself with making small talk as they sauntered down the long, straight path.

They were within sight of the road now and Lori saw another taxi draw up and a man get out. For a moment he was in shadow, but there was something vaguely familiar about his tall, broad-shouldered figure.

But Lori hardly had time to realise that it was Lewis Brent before Tony suddenly hurried her into a pool of light and said harshly, 'This is what I wanted you for,' and pulled her roughly into his arms, holding her so tightly, and taking her so completely by surprise that she couldn't move. His mouth fastened on hers fiercely, and then he caught both her wrists in his left hand, leaving his right free to roughly yank the strap of her dress off her shoulder and fondle her exposed breast.

Lori tried desperately to break free, but Tony always kept himself fit and he held her body hard against his own so that her struggles merely looked as if she was moving sensuously against him. She heard Lewis Brent's footsteps walking briskly along the path, then hesitate as they came near. Deliberately Tony turned her so that the director was sure to see who it was and exactly what Tony's free hand was doing to her. She heard a sharp exclamation and looked over Tony's shoulder to find herself staring into Lewis Brent's face—a face stiff with disgust. Then he turned his head away and walked sharply on up the path.

It wasn't until his footsteps had faded completely that Tony let her go at last.

'You louse! You knew he was coming. You set this up!' Lori hit out at him with one hand and tried to pull her strap up with the other, tears of frustrated anger in her eyes. 'Why? Why did you do it?'

But he caught her wrist and twisted it cruelly. 'Because you kept me out of work for weeks, that's why, you bitch! As soon as I found out that you were going to be in this film I determined to get even with you for what you did to me!'

Lori stared at him aghast. 'Is it because of you that everyone in the crew's been so horrid to me? What have you done? What have you said about me?'

He laughed jeeringly. 'Oh, I didn't have to start anything, your reputation was already in the dirt without my help. I merely let everyone know that you were everything they already thought you were—and perhaps added a little more mud in the process,' he added tauntingly.

Lori felt herself grow cold and stared up at him. 'What are you saying? What do they know about me?'

He laughed again, thoroughly enjoying himself. 'Just the truth about how you got this part, that's all.'

Lori's voice was little more than a whisper as she said, 'But I was offered the part by the producer. He'd seen my work on television.'

'Oh, sure!' Tony jeered, his handsome face twisted by hate and jealousy. 'The connections you've got with the film industry and you expect anybody to believe that?' He was still holding her wrist and he twisted it again before letting her go.

Automatically Lori began to rub where he'd hurt her. 'If you're referring to my godfather, then you're wrong, totally wrong. I've never taken advantage of his position to further my career. I made it clear to him right at the beginning that I'd either succeed or fail on my own merits, and he's always respected my wishes. Believe me,' she said vehemently, 'if I had had his help it wouldn't have taken me so long to get where I am— but there wouldn't have been any pride in what I'd achieved either. But you knew that! You knew that I've never let Uncle Nick help me.'

'Uncle Nick!' He made the name sound like something dirty. 'I know you've said he's never helped you, but everyone here knows that he threatened to withdraw his company's backing for the film unless you were given the part.'

'But that's impossible,' Lori retorted. 'The producer of *The Siege* assured me that it was his own private company making the film.'

'Oh, don't pretend to be naïve,' Tony said sarcastically. 'How could a small film company produce an epic like this without backing from one of the major companies? And your Uncle Nick, as you call him, just happens to be the Executive Vice-President of that company!'

Lori was visibly shaken by this, but was adamant in

her protestations. 'I tell you you're wrong; the producer probably doesn't even know that he's my godfather.'

Tony's mouth twisted into a thin smile. 'You're right, he doesn't. The whole crew, from *Lewis Brent* down,' he emphasised, 'only know that a middle-aged executive insisted that you get the part—perhaps even arranged for the original star to quit just so that you could replace her. *And* overrode all Lewis Brent's suggested alternatives and his objections to working with a completely unknown actress. Seems he even threatened to fire him unless he accepted you,' he went on, his voice silky now. 'But Lewis wanted to do this film so badly, had already been working on the pre-production side for the last six months, that he finally had to accept you—and he didn't like that at all, not one little bit.'

Lori's face had gone very white and her hands had clenched into fists at her sides. She had already foreseen what was coming, but nothing was going to stop Tony from his moment of sadistic enjoyment as he gave her the final blow.

'Naturally everyone wondered just why the Vice-President should be so insistent on having you in the film. And there was only one reason they could think of,' he said nastily. 'That you were his mistress, and he was so besotted by you that he let you persuade him into giving you the part. Or blackmailed him,' he added. 'Quite a few thought it could be that.'

'I see,' Lori said tightly, a feeling of revulsion rising in her stomach at his insinuations. 'And you, of course, didn't choose to enlighten them?'

He shrugged. 'Why should I? I had only your word for it that Nicholas Hayman was your godfather. For all I knew it was true.'

'And the mud you said you added to it? What did your foul little mind come up with?'

The grin was suddenly wiped from his face and he caught her wrist again. 'Don't play the high and mighty with me, you little slut! If you hadn't thought yourself too good to sleep with me I might have befriended you, but as it is,' he paused to let it sink in, 'as it is I told them that you definitely were his mistress, and that you'd willingly go to bed with anyone who would help promote your career.' He bent her wrist back until she had to stifle a moan of pain. 'And for good measure,' he added spitefully, 'I also told them that I'd had you myself, that you begged me to take you because you were so fed up with going with old men. So now every man in the crew thinks he knows exactly what you're like in bed, what tricks you do and what you're good at. I quite enjoyed making that up. I even told them that you....'

But Lori couldn't stand it any longer. 'Shut up! You swine! You're disgusting, do you know that? You....'

Her words broke off in a sharp cry of pain as he bent her arm back viciously. 'Call me names and I'll break your wrist!' He glared at her, then slowly raised his hand to touch her breast again. 'But it doesn't have to be like this, Lori. I could put everything right for you, tell them it was a mistake, that he'd seen your work and knew you were right for the part. I still want you, Lori. All you have to do is say yes.'

Lori heard a car door slam and the sound of several laughing voices coming towards them. She wrenched her wrist free and stared at him. 'I'll see you in hell first,' she said balefully, and then turned to run back towards the safety and light of the hotel.

CHAPTER THREE

THE electronic row from the night-club had little to do with keeping Lori awake that night; she couldn't have slept if she'd tried. She had known that something was very wrong, but never in her worst nightmare had imagined it could be as bad as this. She sat on her bed, leaning against the headboard, her knees tucked up to her chin, and wondered why what she had expected to be one of the most wonderful times of her life had turned out to be a living hell. And she'd only been here a few days!

Her first impulse had been to go to the producer of the film and ask him to tell everyone the truth, but then she thought that if he had heard the rumours he would already have done that. And as he hadn't.... Lori frowned uneasily; it either meant that he hadn't heard the rumours about her, which seemed unlikely when they were the common knowledge of the whole crew, or else he hadn't refuted them because they were basically true and her godfather had got her the part. She stared unseeingly at the opposite wall. Had Uncle Nick broken his solemn word and got her this job behind her back? But if so, why? She had been doing okay on her own, and there had been several tempting offers made to her, including a television serial in the autumn. Despairingly she shook her head. How could she deny anything until she was sure?

And would there be any point in denying it anyway? Her thoughts flew back to that disgusting scene Tony

51

had staged in the garden for the director's benefit. No wonder he had looked at her so contemptuously! After Tony had got through with ruining her reputation, Lewis Brent must have thought she had obliged on every casting couch in London! She felt again his cold eyes flicking over her, and suddenly it became very important that her good name should be restored. Lori laughed aloud, a hollow, empty laugh. Her good name! An extremely old-fashioned way of describing it, but she had never in all her twenty-two years found herself in a situation like this before. Always she had been careful never to get involved in any of the casual relationships that blossomed and died so quickly and so frequently among show business people; you had an affair that lasted for a season or for the length of a show's run, and then the company broke up and everyone moved on to a new show and a new affair. But Lori had never been like that, never been able to give herself lightly to a temporary relationship; always, in her heart, she had been waiting—waiting for what she didn't quite know herself. For a twentieth-century knight in white armour, she supposed, although they seemed sadly out of fashion in this day and age. But the hope that tomorrow or the day after might be the one that brought her ideal had kept her aloof from lesser affairs. And now Tony, in his petty spite, had cheapened and fouled her reputation beyond repair. For Lori knew her show business; this choice piece of gossip would be detailed in every letter home and would be spread throughout the profession in no time at all. And no man who was even halfway decent would want to even look at her!

Very early the next morning, Lori placed a call

through to London and waited impatiently until she was connected.

'Uncle Nick? This is Lori.' The line was bad and she had difficulty in hearing. 'No, I'm all right, but I have to talk to you. Look, there's a rumour going around here that you got me this job. You didn't, did you?' she asked anxiously.

There was a lengthy pause that frightened her before her godfather answered slowly, 'I admit I knew that you were being considered for the part, but I assure you that you got it on your own merit.'

'Oh, Uncle Nick, you're sure? Really sure?' Lori almost began to cry in relief.

'Quite sure,' he replied firmly, then added, 'Why, is there any trouble over there?'

For a moment Lori was terribly tempted to confide in him, to hand her troubles over to him as she had ever since her father's premature death several years ago. He had always been there, to comfort or praise her, and she knew that if she told him the truth he would fly out and try to put things right for her. But whether he would succeed or just add fuel to all the malicious gossip was debatable.

So she merely said as lightly as she could, 'No, it was just a crazy rumour, but I wish you'd do what you could to squash it at your end.'

'Will do.' Lori expected him to question her more closely and was somewhat surprised when he said abruptly, 'I'm going to call on your mother this afternoon. Any messages?'

'My love, of course, but I'll probably phone her myself later.'

He said quickly, 'Oh, I shouldn't do that. I know

she's pretty busy today and all next week. Better if you just dropped her a line. You know she likes getting letters so she can read them over again.'

Lori laughed. 'All right, I'll do that. Love to you both, then.'

But after she had replaced the receiver she stood biting her lip and wondering what to do for the best. The knowledge that Uncle Nick hadn't got her the part was a much-needed boost to her own morale, but wasn't going to alter the crew's attitude towards her one little bit. And in the light of what Tony had told her with such malicious enjoyment she had to decide whether she could go on working in these conditions. Whether she could take three months of being treated like a social outcast, of having the men in the crew looking her over and knowing precisely what they were thinking. And she knew that sooner or later it was inevitable that someone would make a pass at her, thinking her an easy lay, and her rejection of it would only lead to more nastiness.

But she had hardly even begun to work out the problem before the phone rang and she was surprised to hear Lewis Brent's voice.

'Miss West? I'd like you to come down to the production office as soon as possible.'

No would you mind? or please, just a peremptory command that immediately put Lori's back up. And after all it *was* Sunday, she was entitled to her day off, wasn't she?

So she replied coldly, 'Is it important, Mr Brent? I haven't yet breakfasted—and I've made plans to go out for the day.'

His voice grated harshly in her ear. 'Yes, it is important. And the sooner you get down here the sooner you can have the day to yourself. You'll just have to tell your boy-friend to wait.'

And he put down the phone before Lori could even think of a retort.

Grumbling angrily to herself, Lori showered and dressed in a simple sundress and sandals, adding a minimum of make-up. She certainly wasn't going to put herself out for Lewis Brent after the way he'd treated her. So it was in a belligerent mood that she made her way down to the production office and pushed open the door. She had expected to see several people there, but she stood on the threshold and blinked in surprise. The big room was quiet, empty and dark, some makeshift black-out curtains pulled across the windows to shut out the light. For a moment she thought she'd been tricked and there was no one there, but then a light snapped on and she saw the director standing alone on the far side of the room.

'Come in, Miss West, no one's going to bite you,' he said caustically.

Slowly Lori shut the door and walked towards him, wondering grimly whether his bite could possibly be worse than his bark, and why he had sent for her when he was alone. To tell her her work wasn't any good and kick her back to London? Resentment rose in her like an angry tide. He was so prejudiced against her that even if her acting was satisfactory he would still get rid of her. Her chin jutted forward defiantly; she had got this part on her own merits and she was going to fight to keep it.

Lewis Brent watched her as she came towards him, saw the determination in her face and the bright, angry sparkle in her green eyes. For a moment he regarded her in silence, then he motioned towards a couple of chairs. 'Sit down. I want to show you the rushes of your scenes on Wednesday.'

He moved to a projector behind her and turned off the light. Images appeared on the screen in front of her, numbers to show the take and what lenses were used first and then the actual scene. He showed all the takes she had done, the bad ones where she had been nervous or in the wrong position as well as the final one where she had managed to pull herself together and really act. The difference was startling. Lori was ashamed at how appallingly bad she had been at first, and although the final take was far, far better, she wished wholeheartedly that she could take it again; she could see now several points where her performance could have been improved. And if it had been television she would have been able to, because the film would have been processed immediately and run back so that the players could judge for themselves and re-shoot a scene straightaway if they thought they could improve on it, but large screen film processing was far more complicated and always took at least twenty-four hours before the rushes could be viewed, and by then it was often too late to go back; the weather could have changed, the set been pulled down, anything. The actors had to rely completely on the director to get the best performance out of them at the time.

The later scenes were better in that she seemed more assured, and Lori knew that, having seen these rushes, she could improve even more, that it wouldn't take her long to adapt to this new medium given a little help and encouragement, but there was no chance of that with Lewis Brent so dead against her.

As the last scene flickered away, the projector stilled and he turned the light on again. For a few minutes he was occupied with putting away the film, but then he came and hooked forward another chair to sit opposite her. Taking a pack of cigarettes from his pocket, he silently offered her one and when she shook her head lit his own and looked at her consideringly. Lori determinedly kept her mouth shut; he had called her down here, let him do the talking.

After a silence that seemed to stretch to screaming point, he said, 'Well, what did you think of the rushes?'

Lori flushed; did he want her to condemn herself? Acidly she replied, 'What I think of them hardly matters, does it?' Agitatedly she stood up and faced him. 'You'd already made up your mind about me even before you saw the rushes. And now you've got them you're going to use them as an excuse to get rid of me. All right, they were by no means perfect, but with practice I know I could work well in films, I just know I could! But you wouldn't give me that chance, would you?' she added bitterly. 'You're ready to dismiss me out of hand on the basis of my very first day just because I'm not the person you wanted in the part. You're so determined to have your own way that you don't give a damn about anybody else!' she finished, her voice rising.

Lewis Brent regarded her for a long moment, his eyes narrowed against the cigarette smoke, then he deliberately stubbed out the cigarette and said sharply, 'Sit down.'

Lori's mouth tightened mutinously. 'What's the point? You're only going to....'

But she broke off abruptly as he rose and, putting his hands on her shoulders, thrust her down hard into the chair.

'I said sit down!' He looked at her grimly. 'And now

you're going to shut up and listen to me.' He sat down again, his eyes still on her as if daring her to speak, but even when he was satisfied that she wouldn't, he still didn't say anything straightaway, and then, surprisingly, he asked, 'How old are you?'

She looked at him for a moment, wondering where this was leading, then answered reluctantly, 'Twenty-two.' The corner of his mouth twisted sourly and she could imagine just what he was thinking. She glanced at him and said bitterly, 'All right, why don't you get it over with?'

He raised an eyebrow, his eyes cold again. 'And just what do you expect me to say?'

'That you're firing me, of course. That on the strength of one day's filming you know I'm no good.' Then a thought occurred to her and she sat up straight to say, 'But what about Thursday and Friday's takes; why haven't you shown me those? Could it possibly be because I did better in those?' she asked nastily.

Casually he leant back in his chair and crossed his long legs. 'I wouldn't know, I haven't seen them. The dailies are put on a plane to London every night after filming and then flown back here after they've been developed, the whole process taking forty-eight hours. The dailies,' he added sardonically, 'are the footage generated each day during filming.'

But if he had thought to throw her he was disappointed. Lori said sarcastically, 'How convenient! Well, we certainly can't expect you to wait for them before you get rid of me, can we?'

His brow gathered into a frown. 'Just what makes you so sure that I'm going to fire you?'

She stared at him. 'Because you never wanted me in the part, that's why. You've made that perfectly obvious not only to me but to every single member of the crew, and they've all followed your lead. It wouldn't have mattered if my work had been brilliant, you'd still have been determined to get rid of me.' She had to blink back tears and her voice grew husky as she swept on, 'Well, I don't care what you've been told about me or what you think of me, I only know you're unjust and un- fair. But at least getting fired has one big advantage,' she added acidly, 'now I won't have to go through the living hell of having to work with *you* for three months!'

His grey eyes glittered at her angrily and he said sharply, 'Now let me tell you something, Miss West. It's quite true that I didn't want you in *The Siege*, not only because you used unfair means to get the part, but also because this film means a lot to me; the original idea was mine and I did all the research and wrote the outline for the screenplay. I've spent every spare minute I've had in the last three years trying to get backers, assembling the best crew I could find, and per- suading actors who I thought were right for the roles to take part. And then my female lead gets enticed away to another picture and I'm told that I've got to have you or the whole deal falls through. Three years of solid work and sweat wasted and the whole thing to begin again. Have you any idea of the work a director puts into a film?'

Lori shook her head dumbly, impotent in the face of his anger.

He stood up and glared down at her, then began to pace up and down like a caged animal. 'Making a film is blood, sweat and tears. It's a year of unbelievably hard work, of continuous problems that have to be sorted and settled, especially if the film is made entirely on location, as this one is. And a director doesn't just give creative impact to a film, he has to understand what it takes to get a film made—not just artistically, but in nut and bolt production terms. He has to know enough about every job that goes into making a film— from the scene shifter to the sound recorder—so that no expert can override his decision. He *is* the film, it's his creation.'

He stopped and stood staring down where she shrank into her chair. 'And I was supposed to risk all that, risk having the film ruined, just to satisfy the ambitions of the backer's girl-friend!' He leant forward suddenly and put his hands on the arms of her chair, glowering at her so that she jerked her head back. 'But believe me, I would have willingly given it all up, dissociated myself from the film completely and let some other director take over rather than be forced into using someone who would make *The Siege* a lesser film than I'd intended. I don't like blackmail or coercion, Miss West, and I don't like the people who use them.' This latter said so contemptuously that she was left in no doubt at all that he was referring to her.

He straightened and went on coldly, 'But I was told that you could act, and you do bear some resemblance to my first choice, so I eventually agreed to give you a trial. So you see, Miss West, far more than your own future was waiting on the outcome of these rushes.'

Lori stared up at him as he towered over her. 'What —what are you saying?'

'I'm saying that I was amazed to find that you do indeed have a little talent. And with a great deal of hard work and dedication you might eventually be worthy of the part you gained in such a dirty, underhanded way.'

'You mean—you mean you're not going to fire me?' Lori was so stunned by this piece of news that she hardly took in the rest of his words.

'No, I'm not. But before we go into details about your work, I want you to know this. As far as I'm concerned your private life is your own. I couldn't care less who you go to bed with, whether it's the young actor you were with yesterday or the foreigner I saw you going up to your room with the other night, but I....'

'Now just a minute,' Lori burst in angrily. 'I just happened to be waiting for an elevator with the man, nothing more. And as for Tony Rodgers—well, he....'

But Lewis Brent interrupted her sneeringly. 'Do you always laugh and joke with men you meet by the elevators?' He gave an impatient movement of his hand. 'It's nothing to me either way. All I want to get through into your head is that I won't tolerate you creating rivalries among the men in the cast or in the crew so that it interrupts production of the film. Heaven knows, the members of a film crew on location are never very saintly at the best of times, but when a woman of your reputation is available it's asking for trouble. So I warn you now, confine your—activities to just one man or else to men outside the film. I don't want sexual jealousy on my set!' he finished bluntly.

Lori's hands tightened in her lap as anger swept through her like an uncontrollable fire. 'How dare you speak to me like that? You're completely wrong about me. I don't go with men. I'm not....'

'No?' The scorn in his voice lashed like a whip. 'The way you were responding to Tony Rodgers and letting him handle you almost in public didn't exactly strike me as being the actions of an innocent little virgin!'

Lori stared at him in appalled consternation as she

realised that nothing she could say would alter his opinion of her. Circumstances and Tony's spitefulness had combined to damn her utterly in his eyes, and even if she behaved like a nun during the rest of the film, he would still think her cheap and immoral. And that he should think so hurt unbearably. She bit her lip and looked away, unable to bear the derision in his face.

'Quite,' he said coldly, mistaking her action for guilt. 'And now can we forget about the way you *mis*-conduct your life and get down to teaching you some of the techniques of film acting as against those of the stage and television. Now, your biggest fault is that you're pitching your voice as if you're playing to an audience. In a film your only audience is the camera and the microphone boom, and they're only a few feet away, ready to catch even a whisper. Look, I'll put the rushes on again and show you what I mean.'

Lori was still glaring at him angrily, but there was nothing she could do; she just had to grit her teeth hard and try to forget his insults, to concentrate her mind entirely on what he was telling her. And because he was now completely impersonal and businesslike she found this much easier than she had anticipated. The next two hours flew by as Lewis patiently went through each scene with her, telling her where she had gone wrong and giving her advice and tips on how she could improve her performance. She found that he was expert at his job, his knowledge gained from years of studying and experience in the film industry. He taught her a great many things that she knew she might never have learnt by herself and he gave her the sort of help that was going to be invaluable to her during the next three months. It was the help and encouragement she had been crying out for, and if it had been anyone else,

Lori would have been humbly grateful for his instructions and guidance, but when the session eventually came to an end she found that she was unable to even thank him, knowing as she did that he had done so not to help her but simply to make his precious film that much better by her improved performance.

As she gathered up the copious notes she had made, he said, 'I won't schedule you for any scenes tomorrow so that you can think about what I've told you.' And when she didn't answer he added rather caustically, 'All right, you can go now. We mustn't keep your latest lover waiting, must we? But don't worry, you're far too beautiful for anyone to stand you up. But you know that already.'

Anger flamed her cheeks and her eyes. She opened her mouth to let fly at him, but then closed it firmly. What was the use? Turning on her heel, she walked out of the office without another word. And she had been back in her room and studying her notes for quite some time before she suddenly remembered that he had called her beautiful!

The rest of the day Lori spent in solitary pleasure by the pool, writing to her mother, reading, and occasionally dozing in the sun, and that night, because the night-club was closed, she had her first good night's sleep since she'd arrived in Rhodes, waking feeling refreshed and revitalised. She jumped out of bed, determined to make the most of her day off. As yet she had seen nothing of the island except the road between the hotel and the location set in the old city, and she had made up her mind that today she was going to act the tourist and really explore. So she rushed through breakfast and then ran down to the main road to push her way on to a bus already crowded with people going to work or shop in Rhodes town. And the bus in itself was a novel experience. A smiling Greek woman lifted her small child on to her lap so that Lori could sit down, and after she had paid her fare she looked round and saw that there were pictures of local football teams stuck on the sides of the bus, often with coloured rosettes alongside them. The driver's windshield was gaily decorated with a fringed and tasselled pelmet in red and yellow, with a small icon and a pair of miniature football boots dangling from the centre, and what looked like photographs of every member of his family for the last three generations, plus several film stars, inserted into the bottom edges. Everyone was gossiping and laughing, calling greetings to each other down the length of the bus, and generally providing a vivid contrast to the taciturn unsociableness of its British counterpart.

Lori enjoyed it all immensely and was sorry when they reached Rhodes and everyone got off, but before her rose the ramparts of the old city and she eagerly joined the throng of tourists who made their way to a narrow road leading to one of the gateways of the mediaeval town.

Both sides of the road were lined with stalls selling souvenirs, everything from toy Greek soldiers to colourful ceramics, and Lori paused to buy an English edition of a guide to the island. Armed with this, she read that the gate she was about to enter was the Porte d'Amboise, which was guarded on either side by two massive, semi-circular towers which descended to the moat. Lori paused to take a photograph and then turned to look out over the wide, dry moat and to her delight saw several small, tawny-coloured deer roaming there at will, cropping the sparse yellow grass and taking no notice at all of the people crossing the bridge above them. That wild animals could graze so contentedly here amazed her, and she flipped through the pages of her guide book until she found a paragraph explaining that the deer had been adopted as the symbol of Rhodes because in earlier times the old town had been plagued by adders who lived in holes worn into the volcanic tufa stone of the walls, but it was found that the snakes couldn't stand the smell of a deer near them and had to come out of their holes and then the deer stamped on them and killed them, so saving the city. Lori also read that statues of deer now stood on two tall pillars at the entrance to Mandraki harbour, exactly where the Colossus was supposed to have been built.

Lori promised herself a later visit to see them and went through the gateway into the old town, resisted the blandishments of an artist to draw her portrait there and then for three hundred drachmas and went on to the Palace of the Great Magister or Grand Master, who, rather like the Pope, had been elected by the Knights and held the office until he died. This was an imposing building, but a fairly recent reconstruction, which she didn't find very interesting, but when she entered the Hospital of the Knights she immediately felt that she had gone back five hundred years. For the first time it struck home to her forcibly that the Order of the Knights of St John of Jerusalem had been principally founded to maintain a hospital in Jerusalem for pilgrims to the Holy Land, only later taking part in the Crusades and assuming a military character, but always they had maintained a hospital and Britain's own St John Ambulance Brigade was their direct descendant.

Lori stood quietly in the huge ward of the hospital

and gave her imagination full play as she pictured the room lined with cot beds, the nursing brothers moving quietly among the patients, the sun shafting through the high windows in summer, a blazing fire of tree logs in the massive fireplace at the far end of the ward in winter. All along the inner wall there were arched recesses at intervals, and Lori wondered if the dying were taken there to spend their last moments in comparative peace and privacy, while across the room, in the small Gothic chapel built out over the street, the chaplains prayed for the repose of their souls.

The rest of the building was now a museum filled with ancient Greek and Roman artefacts found on the island, but Lori gave this a miss for the present and went instead to find the Street of the Knights because she knew that the film company would be shooting several scenes there in the coming weeks. She didn't know quite what she had expected the street to be like, but nothing could have prepared her for the feeling of timelessness when she came to the bottom of the street and stood looking up its long, straight expanse. If it hadn't been for the people in their bright summer clothes, it would have been exactly like landing in a time machine and stepping into the Middle Ages. The whole street had been preserved exactly as the Knights had left it on the day the remnants of them marched out of the city after having withstood the Turks for six months, and then only being beaten because of the treachery of one of their own number.

Lori wandered slowly up the narrow cobbled street, gazing in awe at the heavy wooden doors under gothic arches leading to the Inns of the five hundred Knights, divided by their various languages or tongues: the Tongue of France, of Italy, of Provence, of Germany and Castile, eight in all. She glimpsed open staircases rising to the upper floors and longed to be able to explore inside, but behind the mediaeval façade the ancient rooms were now lived in by large families of stout women in black dresses and head-scarves, and olive-skinned, curly-haired children who ran barefooted where the feet of the cream of European nobility had trod, and scrawny cats sprawled in the sun on the crenellated roofs where the flags of mighty nations once had flown.

For a long time Lori wandered through the old castle and the town, and with every moment she was filled with the magic of the place, realising just why Lewis Brent had been inspired to make his film, to tell the story of some of the bravest men who had ever fought and died for what they believed in.

As the sun rose higher in the sky, the heat radiated from the stone walls and cobbled, twisting streets where no breath of wind could reach to relieve it. Her senses satiated by history, Lori found a small restaurant nestling under the walls of a mosque built by the Turks during their occupation of the island, and sat down at an outside table in the shade of one of the few trees in the town. She enjoyed herself trying to translate the menu, but finally played safe and ordered moussaka, a traditional Greek dish, with a side salad and a glass of wine. It felt good to sit and relax and just watch the world go by; she had needed this rest to recover from the strain and anxieties of the last few days. She would be better prepared now to face whatever the film crew threw at her, especially since Lewis Brent, however grudgingly, had given her the help she needed.

Thinking of him made her take out her notes and she went through them again, although she already knew them almost off by heart. She tried to relate them to her own performance and was deep in concentration while she ate, but presently she noticed a couple of men from the film crew, wearing *The Siege* tee-shirts, looking into a tourist shop on the other side of the square. Hastily Lori put on her sun-specs, preferring to remain an anonymous member of the public on her day off. But she needn't have worried; the men saw a couple of pretty young girls, Scandinavian tourists from the almost white-blonde of their hair, walking down the street, and immediately turned towards them, ostentatiously displaying their tee-shirts. The girls saw them at once and nudged one another excitedly, then stopped, and Lori heard one say, 'Oh, please. You are in the film?' The men nodded condescendingly, making the most of their claim to fame, and soon all four of them were chatting away and moved off together down the street.

Lori watched them go, an amused smile on her lips. So *that* was why all the men wore the special tee-shirts, because it made it so much easier to pick up girls. The opposition hardly stood a chance. She couldn't recall what jobs the men did in the film company—with a crew of over two hundred it was hardly likely that she would—but she could well imagine the lines that the poor girls were being spun. And the men were probably having a great time in Rhodes; the pick of the prettiest girls, and then finding new ones every two weeks when their package tour ended and the girls flew home.

She sat for a while longer, then paid her bill and walked towards the outskirts of the town where she knew that some scenes were being filmed today. She found the place easily enough, because a largish crowd

had already gathered to watch. There were quite a few
tourists among them, but most of the spectators were
native Rhodians, men too old to work, women taking
time off from household chores, and dozens of children,
all slim and dark, with large, melting brown eyes. Lori
eased her way round the crowd until she found a vantage point and could see clearly, for once a spectator
instead of a participant.

The scene was being shot near the harbour gate and
was of a parley between the Knights and the Turks.
Lori recognised Dean because he had his helmet off,
there being a break in filming, and then she saw Lewis
Brent moving from one camera to another, making sure
the shot would be set up as he wanted it, going over
the moves with the actors, having the lights adjusted to
make sure no shadows were thrown, checking and
double-checking each detail; making absolutely sure
that he got the best acting, the most authentic setting,
perfect camera work. As Lori watched she began to
realise just how hard and indefatigably he worked. He
didn't made a film, he created it. Giving of himself un-
stintingly because it was something he believed in,
something he would never be happy with if it was in
even the slightest degree less than the realisation of his
dream.

And Lori began to feel very humble, realising now
just what it must have meant to him to have her thrust
upon him. She might hate him for his attitude towards
her, his stubborn refusal to even listen to anything she
tried to say in her own defence, let alone believe it, but
she knew now that she respected him and admired his
complete dedication to his work. She found herself ex-
periencing a strange longing to please him, by giving
the best performance of her life and to try to help

make *The Siege* the brilliant picture that he envisaged
—whether she would ever be able to tolerate him as a
man was another question entirely.

CHAPTER FOUR

LORI had made up her mind to give of her best for the
film, but she would have been made to anyway, for
during the next two or three weeks Lewis Brent worked
her hard, giving her only one or two scenes to do per day,
but expecting an extremely high standard and not being
satisfied until he got it. And although he was still harder
on her than any of the other actors, he treated her now as
a director should, encouraging her, and taking her aside
to give her advice instead of doing so in front of everyone. Whether he was pleased with her or not she didn't
know, but although he still told her off when she made a
mistake his voice had lost its sarcastic edge and he no
longer let his contempt for her show.

She found the work tough, admittedly, the immense
concentration and emotion it required often left her
feeling drained, but it was also rewarding and immensely stimulating. She soon found that she was able
to follow his directions imaginatively and almost intuitively, once or twice even daring to tentatively offer
a suggestion of her own. He had turned these down, as
it happened, but not without considering them seriously and telling her why they wouldn't work, usually
because of some technical difficulty.

The crew, too, had become less antagonistic in their
attitude; now someone brought her a lunch-box every

day, and a canvas chair with her name on it had mysteriously appeared on the set one morning. She had been careful, so terribly careful, not to be anything more than friendly with any of the men in the crew, never showing any favouritism to any in particular, terrified lest someone might think she was encouraging them—or, more to the point, that Lewis Brent might think she was encouraging them. Even when Dean came to casually throw himself into a chair beside her and talk shop, asking her what it was like to work on television in Britain and telling her about his own experiences in America, she couldn't enjoy the conversation because she was always worried about the director's reaction.

But strangely enough he didn't seem to mind her talking to Dean at all, often telling them to discuss a scene that they were both in, or strolling across to have a word with them. Lori would look up at him rather nervously whenever he did so. He seemed to tower so tall over her; she always felt as if she wanted to get on her feet to face him, so lessening the advantage he had over her.

Once she laughed aloud at some anecdote Dean had told her and the director looked quickly across and then came over to where they were sitting. Lori stopped laughing abruptly and gripped the arms of her chair, waiting for him to make some biting comment. But he merely looked down at her rather enigmatically and said, 'Dean, can you go and stand in position for a minute so that they can make sure you'll be in camera frame?' Then he turned to Lori and said quietly, 'Relax. I'm not going to eat you.'

Lori gazed up at him uncertainly, unable to read his mood. 'Can I—count on that?'

A faint flicker of amusement came into his grey eyes. 'Just so long as you continue as you are.'

'You mean with my work?'

His mouth thinned. 'I mean with everything.'

'I see,' Lori answered rather shakily.

'I hope you do.' He continued to look down at her for a few moments until Dean rejoined them, then he turned to the younger man and said, 'I shan't need you two any more today. We won't shoot that scene until tomorrow when the sun is rising. Why don't you take Lori up to see the Acropolis and the Stadium? I'm told they're very impressive.'

Lori came slowly to her feet. 'Did I just pass some sort of test?'

Lewis Brent turned to find her green eyes regarding him steadily. 'A test?'

'You just called me by my first name,' she reminded him.

'Did I? In that case I suppose I shall have to keep on doing so.' His expression betrayed nothing, not annoyance with himself because her name had just slipped out, or, alternatively, any degree of friendliness towards her because he had accepted her at last as one of his crew. Usually Lori was good at reading faces, she had the actor's trained eye for it, but his face was like a closed mask. 'You'd better cut along; Dean's waiting,' he added.

Suddenly Lori was angry because she still didn't know what he was thinking. She tossed her head, the red-gold in her hair catching the sun's rays and turning it into a flame. Pertly she retorted, 'Thank you—Lewis.'

For a moment his face tightened and then he turned abruptly and walked away.

Dean whistled up one of the taxis that always hung around near the set and the grinning driver took them out of the town at a fast pace, the rather tinny vehicle rattling along so that Lori was thrown against Dean as they swayed round the bends. He laughed as she apologised, and put an arm round her to steady her.

'These cabs are really something, aren't they? Not that I mind at the moment,' he added with a grin as he held her closer when they made a sharp right turn and started up a steep hill outside the town.

Lori laughed too, but moved away as soon as the car straightened up, holding on to the door to keep herself from falling against him again. If Dean noticed, he didn't say anything, and soon the taxi drew up at a bare strip of ground with just one or two trees casting a meagre shade from the sun.

Dean frowningly handed over what looked to be a lot of drachmas for such a short ride and Lori immediately said, 'Oh, here, let me pay my share,' and dived in her bag for her purse.

But he wouldn't let her, saying, 'No way. It just bugs me that they all overcharge everyone in the film crew. They think we're all millionaires.' He looked around. 'Now, where are these ancient ruins Lewis thinks we ought to see?'

They walked further on and then Lori stopped with a gasp of delight; they were very high up at the top of a steep hill and below them the town of Rhodes was set out like a three-dimensional street map. Lori paid scant attention to the more modern part of the city, turning to study the old town where the Grand Master's Palace stood out clearly, surrounded by the domes and minarets of the later mosques. From this vantage point she could also see where the harbour walls at Mandraki stretched out like long piers into the sea, one of them crowned with three mediaeval windmills, each with their eight thin white sails turning slowly in the sea breeze, all that were left now of the many mills that had stood near the sea when the Knights had held the island. Because all her thoughts now were coloured by *The Siege*, Lori wondered how Lewis would transform the harbour when the time came to film the arrival of the Turkish ships. But it was difficult to think of the director by his Christian name. Her feelings towards him were still very mixed; in his professional capacity she greatly respected him and wanted to please him, but as a man. . . . Emotion governed her senses even when she thought about him, because although he wasn't rude to her any more, Lori could sense intuitively that he still despised her, and her resentment of his attitude was only thinly buried beneath a fragile veneer for the sake of the film. It was as if they had both made a tacit agreement that the film came first, that he would tolerate her because of it, and she would hold her temper in check for the same reason. She could only hope that things would go on as they were, as a gradually improving working relationship, for she hated to think of the explosion that would erupt if she ever did tell him what she thought of him.

'A drachma for your thoughts,' Dean's voice interrupted her, and she turned rather guiltily to look at him.

'I was thinking about the film,' she admitted.

'Then stop it. We came up here to absorb some culture, remember? The wonders of ancient Greece. Let's go find them.'

He took her hand and ran with her across the grass, Lori laughingly telling him to slow down, but he

wouldn't stop until they came to the ruins of the Acropolis where goats cropped the sparse grass among the
scattered stones. Lori's first reaction was of disappointment; all that was left of what had once been a huge
temple to Apollo was just a couple of restored pillars
which gave little indication of the former grandeur of
the building.

Dean saw her disappointed look and said, 'The one
at Lindos is supposed to be much better. Have you seen
it yet?'

Lori shook her head. 'No, I haven't seen any of the
island except Rhodes.'

'Well, we're due to do some shooting there eventually, so we'll see it then. But—hey, why don't we hire a
car on our next day off and go there by ourselves, ahead
of the crew?'

Lori gave him a rather uncertain smile. 'Well, I'd
like to, of course, Dean, but I....'

'But you've got someone else you'd rather go with.'
He gave a slight shrug. 'Sure, I understand.'

He went to turn away, but Lori impulsively put a
hand on his arm. She liked Dean and she didn't want
him to have a bad opinion of her. 'No, it isn't that. It's
just that—well, Lewis warned me to keep away from
all the men in the crew. He—he didn't want me to get
too friendly with anyone, if you see what I mean?'

Dean's handsome face broke into a broad grin. 'Oh,
sure, I know what you mean.'

Lori frowned crossly. 'No, you don't. The rumours
about the way I got this job and—and the other things
that were said about me—well, they just weren't true.
But Lewis wouldn't believe me when I denied them
and told me not to get involved with anyone.' The
memory of that interview still filled her voice with

bitterness. 'So perhaps it would be better if we didn't go out together, even if it is only sightseeing.'

Dean shrugged and said, 'Okay, if that's the way you want it, but if that's the case why did he suggest we come up here together?'

Lori frowned and shook her head. 'I've no idea.'

'I have.' Dean looked at her, his eyes wide and innocent, a saintly expression on his face. 'It's because he knew that my reputation is above reproach, that, like the knights of old, I've taken a vow of chastity, that no woman would ever.... Hey!' He let out a yell as Lori gave him an indignant shove that made him start to slither down the grassy bank, his arms windmilling as he strove to keep his balance.

He recovered quickly and made a grab for her, but Lori laughingly ran away and he didn't catch up with her until she stopped at the entrance to the old stadium and gazed about her in awe.

'Now this really *is* impressive,' she said as she looked down the long, long, length of the oval stadium, flanked by rows of stone seats where the audience had sat. 'What sort of events did they have here? Chariot racing?'

'I think that was the Romans. No, they had athletic meetings, like the early Olympic Games. Some really great athletes were supposed to have come from Rhodes and must have taken part here.'

'How do you know so much about it?' Lori demanded.

Dean grinned. 'I'm an American; I devour guide books for breakfast.'

Lori laughed and walked further into the stadium. 'It must have held hundreds of people. Can't you just imagine them cheering, the men in their skirted tunics, the women in their....'

'Uh-uh.' Dean shook his head. 'No women. They weren't allowed in on pain of death.'

'And why not?' Lori demanded indignantly, her female equality antennae rising. 'I suppose they thought the women would spoil their fun or something?'

Dean grinned. 'No, they were just respecting their modesty. You see, all the men taking part were always completely naked!' And he burst out laughing at her look of shocked surprise.

They spent another hour at the site, exploring the stadium and then the restored theatre where they had fun taking it in turns to stand at the base and declaim all the passages of the ancient Greek plays they could remember, and pulling each other's performances to pieces unmercifully in the style of modern theatre critics.

Lori enjoyed the afternoon immensely and the few hours away from the film helped her to relax and feel less strained. And now that Dean was openly friendly towards her, so the crew's attitude subtly changed and they too began to treat her as one of themselves, so that when Dean asked her to go out with him and some of the others one evening, she had little hesitation this time in accepting. About ten of them, seven men and three women, piled into two taxis and escorted by Janos Karousos, the film company's local contact who was the go-between with the Greeks, went to a night-club called the Copacabana which was patronised entirely by the native Rhodians and tourists were only allowed in as guests when accompanied by a Greek.

The night-club was quite unlike anything Lori had expected; it was a big warehouse-like building with plain wooden tables and benches, the drinks just a bottle of whisky, a bottle of water and half a dozen bottles of Coke per table, take it or leave it. But if the building was primitive, the entertainment was great. Act followed act without a break, singers, dancers, groups of musicians, all came and went on the brightly lit stage and the audience showed their appreciation not by clapping but by throwing carnations to the women and—to Lori's astonishment—throwing piles of plain white china plates to the men, so many that after every popular act boys with wide brooms had to come and sweep away the debris of broken pottery.

Lori sat next to Dean during the course of the evening and he kept trying to refill her glass with whisky, despite her protests. She didn't like whisky very much and kept topping up her glass with Coke to drown the taste, but Dean had no such inhibitions and drank his almost neat. As the night progressed he kept buying more and more piles of plates to throw and insisted that the Greek, Janos, introduce him to many of the locals, going over to the different tables to shake hands and talk and laugh loudly through his interpreter. The Greeks seemed to accept this intrusion good-naturedly enough, but later, when Dean was again back at their own table, he started to whistle and shout for more to an act he particularly liked and several Greeks at near-by tables looked round in open disapproval.

One of the other men at their table stood up. 'Time to take the Golden Boy home. Let's go.'

Dean started to protest vociferously, but they pulled him to his feet and hurried him outside, the rest following.

Lori found herself wedged in a taxi next to one of the women and asked embarrassedly, 'Is Dean always like this?'

The woman gave a shrug. 'He just gets over-friendly when he's had a few drinks, that's all. He likes to think of himself as everybody's best buddy. It doesn't matter so long as we're in a crowd, he always gets taken back to the hotel before he goes too far.'

Lori fully expected Dean to be at least a bit embarrassed at his behaviour, but he turned up at the set the next morning his usual rather brash and friendly self, not in the least bit abashed—and he didn't even have a hangover!

'Hey, we had a great time last night, didn't we?' he exclaimed as he came up to her and put an arm casually across her shoulders. 'Let's do it again. How about tonight?'

Lori was acutely conscious of the whole crew watching them with avid interest and hastily fobbed him off.

'I have an early call tomorrow. Maybe some other time.'

His style of living was too fast for her, she couldn't take that pace every night when she was working, but she did go out with him again two or three times, but always with other people from the film company, not only because there was safety in numbers as far as her reputation was concerned, but also because she was quite sure that she wouldn't be able to handle Dean alone.

So she mostly kept to the hotel in the evenings, forming the habit of learning her lines for the next day's shooting before the night-club opened and then going down to the beach for a late night swim to tire herself physically before going to bed. One Saturday night she had left her swim rather later than usual because she had been writing to her mother, and it was almost one in the morning before she came out of the water and put on her full-length towelling beach robe, knotting the belt loosely at the front. The hotel was still ablaze with light as coaches pulled up at the entrance and deposited an influx of tourists who had spent the night at a 'typical' Greek evening, especially arranged for them at one of the inland villages twice a week and where they all got very merry on the local wine. There also seemed to be a large crowd of local youths hanging around the entrance, so Lori waited until the road was clear and then ran across to go back to the hotel through the gardens.

It was a perfect Mediterranean night; the moon a newly minted silver dollar in the velvet blackness of the sky, the air filled with the scent of the jasmine trees that lined the walk. Lori paused for a moment to let her senses drink it in, but then she froze, nerves quivering as she heard a twig snap and leaves rustle as someone pushed aside the bushes on her left and came towards her.

She made a compulsive movement to start to run, but then stopped as a voice said in an urgent undertone, 'Lori! Lori, wait, please!'

She looked towards the bushes uncertainly, still poised on the edge of flight. 'Who is it?' she said sharply.

'Quiet!' The voice came as a commanding whisper out of the darkness. 'It's me—Dean.'

'Dean? But why on earth....' She crossed the path and went towards him, pushing the screening bushes aside. He was leaning back against the trunk of a palm tree and his face looked pale, sort of washed out, but it could have been a trick of the moonlight. He was slumped against the tree, leaning his whole weight on it, and looked as if his legs might give way at any

moment. Her first thought was that he had been drinking again and she looked at him in some annoyance.

'What happened this time? Why didn't the others
bring you home? Honestly, Dean, you're not safe to be
let out alone!'

He gave her a somewhat ghastly grin. 'I guess you're
right. We got separated—and then—I got into a fight
over some girl.'

He seemed to find it difficult to speak and Lori
thought that he must be really drunk; she hadn't seen
him as bad as this before and just hoped that he wasn't
going to pass out on her.

He had paused for a moment, his eyes closed, his
hand pressed against his side as if he had a stitch. Then
he opened his eyes and looked at her. 'I'm sorry, Lori,
but you're going to have to help me. I'm bleeding like
a pig!' And he slid down the tree trunk and sat on the
ground with a thud.

Lori stared at him uncomprehendingly for a moment,
hardly taking in what he had said until she saw the
dark stain spreading across his shirt. Then she was on
her knees beside him, instinct making her use her towel
as a pad to put against his side and try to stop the bleeding.

'Don't worry, you'll be okay now. Just stay here and
I'll run to the hotel for help. They'll....'

'No!' Dean's urgent exclamation broke in on her
hasty reassurances. 'The people I was in the fight with
—they're waiting at the hotel—I saw them—that's why
—that's why I waited—till someone I knew came
along.' He lay back against the tree, exhausted by his
effort to talk.

Lori gazed at him in consternation. 'But what are we
going to do? Dean?' But the effort had been too much

for him and he had fainted. 'Oh, no!' She bit her lip, wondering what on earth she was going to do, remembering the crowd of youths she had seen at the hotel entrance. Well, one thing was for sure, she had to have help and quickly, there was no knowing how badly Dean was hurt or how much blood he had lost already. She wedged her towel against his side, using the weight of his arm to hold it in place, then pulled some branches across to make sure that he wouldn't be seen by anyone walking home through the gardens. Then she began to run towards the hotel, fear for Dean's life speeding her on.

She had hoped that the garden entrance to the hotel would be clear, but two dark-haired young Greeks were leaning against a wall smoking. For a moment she hesitated, then turned quickly and ran round to the front entrance. Right now she needed the help of someone with enough authority with the hotel management to get rid of the crowd of Greeks—and she knew only one person who carried that much weight. Without hesitation she took an elevator up to the first floor where she knew that Lewis Brent had a suite of rooms. But as she stepped out of the elevator she was dismayed to see several more youths hanging around in the corridor and she remembered that Dean was also living on this floor; the men must be waiting in case Dean somehow managed to get into the hotel and make for his room. Lori shuddered; Dean had really opened up a hornets' nest, and she wondered just what had happened between him and the girl—presumably a Greek girl, to have roused this much bad feeling.

She tried to walk down the corridor to the director's suite as naturally as she could, not too fast so that they would suspect something. One started to come towards her and she had to dig her nails into her palms to stop herself from turning and running back to the safety of the elevator. Somehow she forced herself to keep going to ignore the youth.

He came closer and smiled at her. 'Hallo, beautiful miss. You going to bed?' He put a hand on her arm. His skin was rough and his nails were dirty. 'You want I should come with you? We Greeks know how to treat a woman in bed.' He came closer and tried to put his other hand on her breast. His breath reeked of alcohol.

Lori drew away in repulsion but inwardly sighed with relief; it was only a pick-up. She brushed him off and hurried down the corridor, the youth turning to watch her. At Lewis's door she knocked loudly, willing him to hurry. The Greek was still watching her as she waited impatiently for Lewis to answer. Then fear shot through her at the thought that he might be out. He could still be at the set, in the production office, anywhere! She tried to think whether there was any night shooting today, but her brain was numb with fear and she couldn't remember. The youth grinned leeringly at her again and started to walk towards her. Lori lifted both fists and beat against the door, yelling 'Lewis!' on a rising note of panic.

'What the hell?' The door was suddenly yanked open and Lori almost fell inside, gasping with relief. She glanced behind her, but the Greek was already hurrying back down the corridor.

'Oh, thank God! I was afraid you weren't here. I didn't know what to do.'

'Lori! What on earth's the matter?'

He was dressed in only a brown terry bath-robe, his hair still damp from the shower.

'It's Dean. Oh, Lewis, you've got to do something!

He's hurt, I don't know how badly, and there are men all round the hotel. Oh, please, you've got to help me!' Her voice rose incoherently and she put up her hands to grip the lapels of his bath-robe, trying to pull him towards the door.

'Wait a minute. You say Dean's hurt? Where is he? What happened?' His hands came up to cover hers, warm and strong, forcing her to keep still.

'He's in the gardens. There's blood all over his shirt. I don't know how bad he is—he could be dying. Oh, please, Lewis, hurry! He's unconscious.'

Lewis's face grew grim. 'Then we're going to need a stretcher.' He moved towards the phone, but Lori caught hold of his arm.

'First you've got to see the manager. He got in a fight with some Greeks and now they're waiting outside in the corridor and at the entrances of the hotel. But you can....'

She broke off abruptly as Lewis caught hold of her wrist, gripping it hard. 'You say he got into a fight?'

'Yes, with a crowd of young Greeks. He....'

'You little tramp!' Lewis's voice was suddenly savage. 'What the hell have you done to him? I should have known that a slut like you wouldn't be happy with just one boy-friend, that you'd enjoy playing one man off against another.'

Lori stared at him open-mouthed, unable to take in that he was blaming her. Before she could speak, he said tersely, 'Wait here,' and disappeared into the connecting bedroom.

He was back in two minutes, dressed in jeans and casual beach shoes and carrying a lightweight sweater. 'Here, hold these.' He tossed her a small first-aid pack and a pocket flashlight while he pulled the sweater over his head. His chest was broad and muscular and in the casual clothes he looked tough and capable. Despite her indignation that he had immediately jumped to the wrong conclusions, Lori was glad that she had come to him, and she knew that he was more than competent to deal with this or any other sticky situation.

'Come on.' Lewis took the things from her and stuffed them in his pocket as they left his room.

The elevator was still at this floor and Lori glanced round quickly as they got into it, but the two men had moved to the other end of the corridor. Nervously she pointed them out to Lewis. 'Those men—I'm sure they're waiting here in case Dean tries to get to his room. Are you going to see the manager? Tell him to get rid of them?'

'I want to see how badly Dean's hurt first,' he answered shortly.

Lori looked at him uncertainly, wanting to tell him that he was mistaken, that Dean had got into a fight over someone else, but his face looked so cold and forbidding that she knew that this just wasn't the time to start making hurried explanations. The elevator came to a standstill and the doors sighed open.

'There are two more Greeks waiting by the garden entrance. Do you see them?'

Lewis gave a quick glance towards the doors and his jaw tightened. 'I see them,' he answered grimly, and then, to her complete surprise, he laughed aloud and put his arm round her waist, drawing her close to him. Lori looked at him in a bemused way and he laughed again and bent his head down to hers. 'Act, can't you?' he hissed in her ear. 'We're going for a moonlight stroll in the gardens. You should know how to play this scene—you've probably done it with a dozen different men since you've been here.'

Lori's back stiffened with rage, but she remembered the need for haste and let him walk her out of the doors and down the steps to the path, the waiting Greeks giving them no more than a passing glance. Lewis continued to hold her until they turned a bend in the path and then Lori immediately pulled away and glared at him balefully.

'If I were a man I'd knock you down for saying that!'

His mouth twisted wryly. 'If you were a man I'd have no cause to say it. Now, where's Dean?'

'Back here.'

Lori led the way through the bushes and they found Dean still slumped against the tree, but he had regained consciousness and gave a grin of relief when he saw them.

'Boy, am I glad to see you two! I was beginning to think I'd have to try and make it on my own.'

Lewis knelt down beside him and gave Lori the flashlight to hold while he began to remove the pad of towel so that he could see the wound. Lori noticed that he was very gentle, causing Dean as little hurt as possible, but even so he gave a smothered groan as Lewis laid bare the wound.

'I guess I really—messed things up this time, didn't I?' he gasped.

'You certainly seemed to have turned the locals against you,' Lewis agreed grimly as he opened the first-aid pack and took out a dressing. 'What was it—a knife?'

'Yeah, they really fight dirty around here.' Dean's voice faltered as he asked, 'Is it—is it very deep?'

'Deep enough,' Lewis replied steadily. 'But I expect we'll be able to patch you up so that you'll be able to finish the film. That's if you don't let yourself get involved in another fight, of course,' he added grimly, his deft fingers fixing the dressing in place. 'But perhaps you've at least learned that it's hardly worth getting yourself punctured full of holes for the sake of a girl, especially a promiscuous little tramp like her!'

The torch wavered at that and Lori would dearly liked to have hit him with it, but if the insult was intended to provoke some remark, it failed; she kept her mouth tight shut. She had a whole lot she wanted to say to Mr Almighty Brent, but now was neither the time nor the place.

Dean managed a weak choking sound of a laugh. 'I really fell for it, didn't I? She looked so sweet and innocent.'

'Oh, yes,' Lewis agreed caustically, glancing up at Lori, his eyes narrowed, adding deliberately, 'To look at her you'd think she was completely untouched, unawakened—until you realise there's only a bed-hopping wanton behind that perfect face.'

What Lori would have said or done at that she never knew, because they heard footsteps coming along the path from the direction of the hotel and Lewis stood up and said swiftly, 'Put out the light!' and they waited in silence until the footsteps had gone safely past.

'What are you going to do?' Lori asked him softly. 'Shall I get a taxi to take him to hospital in Rhodes?'

Lewis shook his head. 'No, he's lost a lot of blood and I'm afraid a ride in one of those tin-can taxis might open up the wound again,' he answered, pitching his voice too low for Dean to hear. 'But the knife must have gone in deep and he could need a transfusion.'

'But you said. . . .' Lori broke off, realising that he had only been trying to reassure Dean. She looked at him helplessly. 'What are we going to do?'

Lewis made up his mind and said briskly, 'We're going to take him into the hotel.'

'But the men?'

'We'll distract them.' He pointed. 'That kaftan thing you're wearing—it's got a hood, hasn't it?'

'Why yes, but. . . .'

'Good. Take it off.'

She goggled at him. 'But I can't! I. . . .'

'You've got something on underneath, haven't you?'

'Of course, but I. . . .'

'Then take it off, woman. Or do you want me to take it off for you?'

Lori glared at him. 'That will *not* be necessary.' She unzipped the robe and stepped out of it, shivering as the cold night air struck her still damp costume.

'Help me get him up.'

Between them they hoisted Dean to his feet, although Lewis had to hold him to stop him from falling again.

'Sorry,' Dean mumbled. 'Everything went round for a minute.'

'Not to worry, old son. We'll soon have you tucked up in bed,' Lewis reassured him, then turned to Lori and said in a completely different tone, 'Don't just stand there; put the kaftan on him.'

Grimly Lori obeyed him, marvelling that his manner could change so completely; he was always so pleasant to Dean and so nasty to her. His eyes met hers and he frowned impatiently so that she hastily lifted the kaftan over Dean's shoulders and helped him put his arms into it.

'Good. Pull the hood down over his head so that no one can see his hair.' He gave Dean a grin of encouragement. 'Okay, let's go.' He stooped and picked Dean up in his arms without apparent effort, although Dean

was big himself and must have weighed over a hundred
and fifty pounds. He carried him through the trees
towards the hotel, only stopping when they got near
enough to see the two youths still standing in the light
from the doorway.

'All right, here's where you start making up for what
you've done,' Lewis said to Lori softly. 'Go and draw
them away long enough for me to get him into the
elevator. And I shall want your room key. Where is it?'

'In the pocket of the kaftan,' Lori replied automatically, adding worriedly, 'But how can I draw them
away? What if they won't move?'

'Oh, they'll move all right, especially when they see
you dressed in that,' he added, his eyes running derisively over her slim figure. 'You know how to lure a
man, none better. Now get on with it.'

Lori gave him one last fulminating look and stepped
out into the sight of the two youths.

She strolled slowly towards them, trying to give herself time to work out a scheme to draw them away; it
was all very well for Lewis to say that she would know
what to do, but she was in a sweat of fear as she got
near to them and still hadn't thought of anything. They
straightened as she approached, their dark eyes running
over her in insolent appraisal. Reluctantly Lori began
to mount the steps to the terrace. What was she supposed to do, for heaven's sake—invite them to take her
into the bushes? Did Lewis really expect that of her?
Presumably he did, when he regarded her as just a
tramp, she realised resentfully. Hate ran through her
like a wave and must have sent some adrenalin to her
brain, because suddenly she knew what to do.

As she reached the terrace she turned sharply away
from the doors, deliberately ignoring the youths and

walking quickly away as if she was going round to the main entrance of the hotel. They looked after her disappointedly, and Lori could imagine with some satisfaction what Lewis's reaction would be as he watched her; he would think that she had chickened out and left him to cope alone. And serve him right if she did, she thought viciously. But there was Dean to think of. With a sigh Lori walked near to the edge of the steps that ran all along the terrace, pretended to catch her foot, and gave a sharp cry of fear that wasn't all pretence as she tumbled down the stone steps.

She felt a stunning pain in her left elbow as it hit hard against a step and then she was lying in a heap on the ground, the hard stones pressing into her bare skin. Behind her she heard running footsteps and one of the Greek youths stooped over her, taking her arm to help her up. But she had to get both of them away from the door. She let him assist her, but when she tried to stand fell down again with a pitiful moan.

'My ankle! Oh, I think it's broken!'

Whether he understood or not, the young man got the message. He tried to lift her, but like most Greeks he was short and slim, and Lori deliberately made herself as heavy as possible, slumping against him and pushing him off balance. Would the other man come? He just had to! She groaned again and pretended to faint. There was a swift interchange between the two men and then the other ran over to help. Between them they picked her up and began to carry her towards the main entrance. Lori gave a silent prayer of thanks. When they were safely round the corner and out of sight of the garden entrance, she let as much time as she thought Lewis would need elapse and then let herself begin to come to. They stood her up and fussed over her, which included patting her all over to see if she was hurt anywhere else; their hands seemed to be everywhere, but they were very polite and solicitous and Lori marvelled at a temperament that could change from young thug to helpful Samaritan within minutes. She assured them that she felt much better, that her ankle had only been twisted and that she could manage, but they insisted on helping her along almost up to the main entrance before they saw the other youths and remembered they were supposed to be standing sentry, then they melted away and left her to go on alone.

Lori hurried on, anxious to get to her room and make sure that Lewis and Dean had reached it safely. A taxi pulled up and some tourists got out, the women giving her disparaging looks as they saw how she was dressed —or undressed, more like. Oh, dear, she'd forgotten that she'd have to walk right through the hotel wearing just her bikini, a thing she wouldn't even do after coming back from the beach in daytime. But there was nothing else for it. Squaring her shoulders, she walked quickly through the main doors, ignoring the tourists, the youths who called after her in admiration, and the startled look of the receptionist at the desk, and made quickly for the elevators. She suffered several minutes of acute embarrassment while she waited, and of course someone tried to pick her up, a fat, florid-faced man who tried several languages and pushed himself up against her quite unnecessarily when the elevator came. The other people in the elevator got out on the lower floors, but he stayed on, trying to paw her, and Lori had to get really nasty and stamp on his foot with her high-heeled sandal before she managed to get away from him at the seventh floor. He shouted something obscene after her and there were tears of anger and resentment in her eyes as she reached her room and knocked on the door.

It was opened a fraction as Lewis looked out and then he opened it wide and let her in. If he noticed her heightened colour he ignored it, merely letting her pass him and go into the room. Dean was lying on one of the beds, his face a ghastly colour in the electric light.

'How is he?' she asked anxiously.

'He passed out again. I've sent for a doctor, he should be here very shortly.' Ignoring her, he crossed to the phone and told the operator to get him the manager. Lori heard him telling the poor man in no uncertain terms to get himself out of bed and get rid of the gang of youths hanging round the hotel.

Going to the wardrobe, Lori took out some clothes and went into the bathroom to change. It was a relief to take off the wet bikini, but as she towelled herself dry the material caught on her elbow and made her wince in pain. Twisting round to look in the mirror she saw that it was badly grazed and oozing with blood. She put on her pants and bra and a clean pair of jeans, then poured some antiseptic on to a pad of cotton wool and tried to clean up the graze.

But as she did so there was a sharp knock on the door and Lewis called out, 'Open up; Dean wants a drink of water.'

Obediently she unlocked the door and moved aside as he went to the sink. He saw the antiseptic bottle and said, 'What's the matter?'

Shortly she answered, 'It's nothing,' and moved her elbow out of his sight.

'Let me see,' he commanded, and put down the glass to catch her arm and pull her round towards him. 'How did you do that? In the fight?'

'I wasn't in any fight. I did it when I pretended to fall down the steps.'

'I thought it was a rather drastic way of distracting them.'

'It was all I could think of,' she said defensively.

He raised his eyebrows in transparent disbelief, then took the wad of cotton wool from her and began to clean up the sore.

'I can manage, thanks.' She tried to jerk her elbow away, but he wouldn't let her, holding it in a firm grip. A sudden wave of impotent anger filled her and she felt an overwhelming urge to lash out at him, if not physically at least verbally. She said coldly, 'You came to get Dean a drink. You mustn't keep him waiting.'

He glanced towards her. 'A couple of minutes won't hurt him.'

Slowly, nastily, keeping her eyes fixed on his, she said clearly, 'That's very big of you. Wasting your time on a woman when you know you'd rather be with a man, especially one as handsome as Dean.'

The grip on her arm tightened convulsively so that she gave a sharp gasp. His dark eyes fastened on hers and she grew cold with fear.

'And just what was that remark supposed to mean?' he demanded harshly, his eyes dark as winter storm-clouds.

Lori knew that she should draw back, take the opportunity he had given her and say it was nothing, but some fatal compulsion drove her on, and even while she stared into his eyes and said, 'You know *exactly* what it meant,' she knew that she had gone too far.

His mouth tightened and a look of such murderous fury came into his eyes that Lori thought he was going to hit her and she instinctively moved away, but he suddenly jerked her hard against him. 'You little bitch!' he said savagely. 'So that's what you think, eh? Well, I'll just have to convince you that you're wrong, won't I?'

Too late, Lori realised what he was going to do—tried to pull away, but he seized a handful of her hair, twisting his fingers in it, not caring that he hurt her, and then, very slowly, he pulled her head back and kissed her. Lori kept her mouth closed, trying desperately to break free, but her struggles were useless against his strength; he only tightened his hold and hurt her more, the pressure of his mouth forcing hers to open. The masculine demand for submission was so strong that for a moment she almost weakened. Lewis must have felt it, for his free hand slipped down to her hips to press her body close against his own while his lips became even more importuning. The hardness of his body sent a surge of sexuality running through her like a fire and at last she opened her mouth beneath his bruising kiss.

He made a small sound of satisfaction as his hand moved up to unhook her bra, but it was enough to bring her crashing back to her senses and she gave a gasp of revulsion as she pulled free of him, her arm quickly going up to hold her bra in place.

For a long moment her green eyes stared into his grey ones, then, her breathing still unsteady, she said shakily, 'All right, you made your point. Now get out of here.'

His eyebrows rose and his mouth twisted in mocking derision, but then he turned to pick up the glass of water and left her alone.

Angrily Lori bolted the door behind him and with

trembling hands put a plaster over the graze on her elbow and finished dressing. Her lips still felt bruised and her eyes were wide and vulnerable when she looked in the mirror. From outside she heard a knock on the door and then a murmur of voices. Quickly she went into the bedroom and saw a doctor leaning over Dean and starting to examine him while Lewis stood nearby. When he saw her he came over to her and took a key from his pocket.

'You can spend the rest of the night in my suite. Here's the key.' His voice was quite impersonal, as if that nasty little scene in the bathroom had never taken place.

Lori hesitated. 'What about Dean?'

'I'll stay with him. Go with him to a hospital if the doctor thinks it necessary.'

Her eyes were troubled as she looked up at him. 'I'd like to stay too. I can take it in turns to watch with you. Please, I feel responsible for him and I'd like to....'

'You *are* responsible,' Lewis interrupted brusquely. He continued to glare at her for a minute, then shrugged, 'All right, you might as well take some of the responsibility for your handiwork. Go and wait on the balcony until the doctor has finished.'

Lori looked up at him resentfully, a tart reminder that this was her room already on her lips, but she had already had one lesson by defying him tonight and she knew she was quite unable to take another. Slowly she lowered her glance and obediently went to wait in the cool darkness of the balcony.

CHAPTER FIVE

RHODES was a strange island; the western coast was bounded by the Aegean Sea which had a strong tide that sent large waves rolling on to pebble beaches and blew fresh winds that made the heat tolerable by day and turned the air chill at night, whereas the eastern side had its feet in the tranquil blue waters of the Mediterranean, where the beaches were long stretches of oven-hot golden sand, the waters were calm and crystal clear and where not a breath of wind came to disturb the intense, dazzling heat. The hotel was situated on the western coast and normally Lori was glad of the breeze, but now it struck cold and she pulled a chair into the furthermost corner of the balcony and huddled into it, her feet tucked under her.

It was very late; she hadn't got her watch on, but she guessed that it must be after two in the morning and she felt terribly tired. The night-club was still in full swing above her, but even the noise of that couldn't keep her awake and she drifted into an uncomfortable sleep. She woke with a start, some primeval instinct telling her that she wasn't alone, and looked up to see Lewis standing over her, a rather bleak look on his face. This disappeared as soon as he saw that she was awake and his face became its usual cold mask.

'The doctor's gone, you can come back inside.'

Lori stretched her cramped muscles. 'What did he say? Was it very bad?'

Lewis shook his head. 'No, he said it was a clean

wound and not too deep, luckily, but Dean's lost a lot of blood and he'll have to have complete bedrest for a couple of days and then take it easy for a week or two.' He went to add something more, but then the band, who must have been between numbers, suddenly blasted into a top rock tune and drowned his words. A look of amazement came over his face and he hastily pulled her inside the room and shut the windows. 'What on earth is that?'

Lori regarded him with some satisfaction. 'It's the night-club, it's immediately overhead.'

'Good God! Does it make that row every night?'

'All except Sundays. It starts at ten and finishes at exactly four in the morning. The Greeks are very punctual,' she added wryly.

'Then we'd better keep the windows shut and turn on the air-conditioning or it might disturb Dean.'

Lori went over to look at Dean, who was asleep, his handsome face very pale on the pillow. 'There isn't any air-conditioning—it only goes up as far as the fifth floor,' she informed Lewis.

'But it's stuffy in here already. How on earth do you sleep?' His expression became cynical. 'But then I don't expect you're here often, you're probably too busy sleeping around in other men's bedrooms!'

Lori was cold and tired, there had been all the stress and worry about Dean, the fear of him being injured further, and then Lewis's contemptuous assumption that it was all her fault. And now at this last insult something seemed to snap inside her. She straightened up and turned to face him, her hair blown into disarray by the wind, her eyes sparkling with indignation.

'How dare you speak to me like that? From the very first, even before I came here, you've listened to and believed every piece of malicious gossip about me. And when I tried to tell you that you were wrong all you did was to virtually laugh in my face! You've been against me from the very beginning, and even though I've kept away from the men in the crew, only going out in a crowd and not even talking to any one man more than another, you're still so completely prejudiced against me that you think you have the right to insult me whenever you want!' Her voice started to rise on a note of hysteria. 'Well, I'm just about sick and tired of your insults, do you hear me? Okay, so you wanted another actress to play the part and you got me instead. Well, that's bad luck on you, but you have no right to treat me like dirt because of it. I didn't ask for this part—it was offered to me. I'm doing my best to play it as you want and I...!' She broke off, realising that she was sinking into pathos, and her mind filled with impotent anger. She lifted her hands in a helpless gesture. 'Oh, what's the use? You're so determined to be convinced that I'm no good that you'll never believe a word I say. You even blamed me for—for Dean when I wasn't even with him!' Tears of tiredness and frustration came into her eyes and she hastily turned her back on him, ashamed to let him see her weakness.

For a moment there was a silence that hung heavily between them while Lori fought to control herself, digging her nails into her palms, determined not to let him see her cry.

At length he said caustically, 'I seem to remember that you handed out some insults of your own tonight.'

Slowly she turned to look at him and found him regarding her grimly. 'I know. It was very wrong of me; I'm sorry. And I knew it wasn't true really, I knew you weren't like that. I suppose—I suppose I just wanted to hit back at you,' she admitted with honest candour.

He frowned. 'And you certainly didn't pull your punches—not to mention hitting below the belt!' Crossing the room, he came to stand close beside her. 'And now you want me to believe that everything I've heard about you is wrong, and that you didn't get Dean into a fight?'

A flash of hope filled her and she gazed up at him pleadingly as he looked at her consideringly. Then his expression changed to one of complete cynicism as he said, 'You know, Lori, you really are a very good actress. For a moment I could almost have believed you.'

The hope died like a trodden ant. 'I'm telling you the truth,' she said wearily. 'Why won't you believe me?'

His mouth tightened. 'Maybe I would have done if you hadn't deliberately provoked me into kissing you earlier. Your power to attract men sexually may be immense, but don't try to play games with me, Lori, because I can see through you at every turn. You thought that if you hooked me I'd forget about what happened to Dean, but if you think I'd fall for someone who uses her beauty as a weapon or a bribe, and who sleeps with every man who comes along, then you're very much mistaken!'

Lori glared at him furiously. 'Don't kid yourself! You're the last person I'd want to attract. I don't go for self-opinionated, pompous bigots—and you certainly don't turn me on!'

'No?' He caught hold of her arm, the grey eyes filled with insolent mockery, and for a heart-stopping moment Lori thought he was going to kiss her again, but he merely gave her a little shake and then said, 'Did you mean it when you said you were willing to sit up with Dean?'

She blinked, strangely unwilling to accept his change of mood. 'Yes. Yes, of course,' she replied after a moment.

'Then stay with him while I go and find the manager and try to smooth things over with the locals. This affair has to be settled somehow or else Dean won't be able to set foot outside the hotel.' He checked that the younger man was still sleeping and then let himself out, taking the key with him.

Lori turned out the main light and lay on the other bed, her ears alert for any sound Dean might make, but she guessed that he had been given a sedative, he slept so deeply, hardly moving at all. She lay back on the pillow and tried to gather her thoughts, but strangely none of them were of Dean; she liked him and was sorry he had been hurt but quite frankly considered that he had brought it on himself; he was far too exuberantly outgoing towards the Rhodians, both male and female, and should have realised that his ways were not theirs and they would resent his being familiar with one of their unmarried girls, who were still chaperoned until marriage.

No, her thoughts were all of Lewis. Lewis, whom she had always considered to be so cold and impersonal until her stupid accusation had shaken him out of his usual aloofness and he had picked up her challenge so rapidly and with such passion that she would never again be able to think of him without remembering it —that and the effect it had had on her. She had been kissed many times before, not only in her private life but also during her work, by handsome men who were

supposed to be sex symbols, by tough anti-hero types,
and by men who were neither of those but just plain
nice. With a few of them things had gone a little deeper
and might have become serious if Lori hadn't always
had this feeling that she wanted to wait; there was
plenty of time, she was in no hurry to tie herself down.
Most of them were well practised in the art of making
love to a woman and had known how to kiss and caress
her, but none of them, not even the most experienced,
had ever inflamed her like that one angry kiss, given
cold-bloodedly and without emotion, used only as a
means of teaching her a lesson. The thought of it made
her tremble and she put a finger up to her lips; they
still felt bruised and tender.

It was well over an hour later before Lewis came
back, letting himself quietly into the darkened room,
but Lori sat up immediately, fully awake but afraid he
might accuse her of having fallen asleep.

'How is he?' he asked.

'Just the same, he hasn't stirred.'

'Good. I'll take over now for what's left of the night.
Go down to my room and sleep there.'

'I don't mind staying,' she offered stiffly.

'I dare say you don't, but I intend to get some rest
on that bed,' he told her bluntly.

'Oh! I see.' She got up and collected her nightdress
and clean clothes for the morning, then took his key
from him. 'What about tomorrow, who will look after
him then?'

'The doctor's arranging for a nurse to come in. And
I've also seen the manager about a new room for you—
you're to have one on the third floor from tomorrow.'

Lori looked at him in some astonishment. 'But when
I asked them if I could change they said they had no

more available until the end of the season.'

Lewis raised a cynical eyebrow. 'Obviously they were more open to high-level pressure than low-level sexuality.'

Her jaw tightened but she said gratefully, 'Thank you; the noise of that band has been driving me mad.'

His mouth twisted derisively and he mocked her own words cruelly, 'Don't kid yourself. I didn't do it for you —I merely wanted this room for Dean until he's well enough to be moved back to his own.'

Lori stared at him bitterly, then turned abruptly and left him to his vigil.

The sound of the phone ringing brought Lori awake in the morning after a long dreamless sleep. She stretched languorously in the big double bed—no lonely single ones in this suite—and reached for the phone on the bedside cabinet. Lewis's voice brought her instantly fully awake.

'I trust you slept well?' he asked drily.

'Your bed is very comfortable,' she agreed.

'Have you any idea what the time is?'

'No. It's Sunday; I never look at clocks on Sundays,' she replied, refusing to be drawn.

'It's nearly eleven.'

'Is that all? In that case I think I'll go back to sleep for a couple of hours.' And she gave an exaggerated yawn. 'Goodbye.'

'Wait!' Lewis' voice came sharply over the line and Lori gave a small smile of satisfaction. 'Look, I want to use my room to shower and change. All your things have been moved from here and sent down to room 327. I'll have the key sent to you.' He paused, then said abruptly, 'And when you're ready I want to talk to you.

I have to go over to Lindos today to look at a site we want to use in the film. We can drive there and talk over lunch.'

Lori gave a gasp at this autocratic command that took it for granted that she would obey him. Indignantly she said, 'What makes you think I haven't got a date for today?'

'Have you?'

She bit her lip. 'As it happens I haven't, but. . . .'

'Phone me at your old room as soon as mine is free. I want to get started as soon as possible.' And he put down the receiver.

Contrarily, Lori took as long as she could to shower and dress; let the man wait, it would serve him right, but when she phoned him at last he merely acknowledged the call and told her to meet him in the foyer in half an hour. Room 327 was filled with sunlight, the heat softly dispelled by the coolness of the air-conditioning. The chambermaid had unpacked for her and all her clothes were neatly arranged in the large wardrobes, but the nicest thing of all was that the room faced the sea. Lori went out on to the balcony and drank in the view. The sky was its usual uninterrupted vastness of intense blue, she hadn't seen a cloud all the time she had been here, and far away on the horizon she could clearly make out the mountains of Turkey, only a few miles away across the sea. It was so close that there used to be day trips there from Rhodes, but now the political situation between the two countries was highly inflammable and she had been disappointed to learn that the excursions had been stopped. Her gaze fell to the gardens and brought her mind back to last night with a sickening jolt. She wondered what Lewis wanted to talk to her about; to throw more insults at her, probably, it was getting to be almost a regular thing. She sighed and turned back into the room. She supposed she'd have to go with the man; he was still the director of *The Siege* and therefore her immediate boss.

But, although she told herself firmly that she couldn't care less what he thought of her, something still made her put on her make-up carefully, brush her hair until it shone, and change into a simple, sleeveless, button-through dress of cream silk with a wide leather belt that accentuated her tall slenderness. A last critical look in the full-length mirror—another advantage over her old room—and she went to meet him, her heart beating unusually fast and a faint flush on her cheeks that owed nothing to make-up.

Lewis was waiting for her in the foyer, dressed in a lightweight beige linen suit with a shirt of a darker shade open at the neck. He turned to look at her as she crossed the wide foyer, as did every other man in the place. Lori was used to the effect she had on men—she could hardly not be—but Lewis's face was completely expressionless as he watched her walk towards him. There was neither the usual look of gratification that most of her escorts wore on seeing her, nor even annoyance that she had kept him waiting so long. Nothing. He merely put on a pair of dark glasses and opened the door for her to go outside to where a hired convertible was waiting. Again he held the door for her, but made no attempt to help her in before silently taking his place beside her and driving away from the hotel.

They had been travelling for over a mile before Lori broke the silence by pointing out tartly, 'For someone who wanted to talk to me you're being extremely reticent.'

His eyelids flickered for a second, but he only said, 'There's plenty of time. Enjoy the ride.'

'I didn't come along for the ride.' Then, when he was silent, 'How is Dean this morning?'

'He's sitting up and eating a hearty breakfast come lunch and trying to get the nurse to teach him Greek.' He smiled, and for a fleeting moment Lori wondered if he would ever smile at her like that.

'I'm glad.' She turned and looked rather blindly out of the window.

The road to Lindos ran along the eastern side of the island, often up hills which gave the most breathtaking views of the Mediterranean, of long, sweeping bays or small coves bounded by rocky cliffs. Inland they passed through villages where the tavernas spilled out on to the street, the tables full of stocky, dark-haired men who played backgammon so fast the counters seemed to move like magic. And everywhere there were tourist shops hung with riots of embroidered blouses, lacy shawls and brightly coloured folk-weave mats with traditional Greek amphorae designs, while others had cotton dresses and kaftans on hangers that were strung one above the other on long poles, to hang from nearby tree branches or to lie in a rainbow of colour against the dazzlingly white walls of the houses. They had to wait to pass a crowd of black-clad women who gathered round a donkey cart piled high with melons and often slowed down to pass weatherbeaten peasants who sat astride already heavily-laden mules and made their way to market exactly as they had before the occupation by the Germans, the Italians, the Turks, the Knights of

St John, the Persians, the Goths and the Romans. A small island that had been invaded and pillaged time and time again throughout history, but which had always maintained its intrinsic Greek nationality.

Their first sight of the ancient city of Lindos was spectacular to say the least; they had been driving along a dusty road between outcrops of seamed volcanic rock where sheep tried to graze on the grass-starved hills or in dried up river beds which wouldn't flow again until the winter rains, and then they topped a rise and found spread out before them one of the most beautiful panoramas Lori had ever seen. She gave an involuntary gasp of delight, and Lewis pulled up at the side of the road to take a longer look. Below them lay a wide bay fringed with sand as white and clean as talcum powder that sloped gently down to the deep blue stillness of the sea. To their left the bay stretched far into the distance, broken only by a few houses surrounded by olive trees, but to their right the town of brilliantly white, cube-shaped houses clustered at the foot of a steep hill, and on top of the hill, like a crouching lion, stood the massive walls of a mediaeval fortress. The white houses stood out starkly against the brown stone, but the castle high above them must have been built from the local rock, for it blended in perfectly with the landscape, only its castellated battlements outlined against the perfect azure blue of the sky.

Lori gazed in awe for several minutes and then turned impulsively to Lewis, her face glowing. 'It's perfect! I've never seen such a beautiful place. Rhodes must be the loveliest island in the world.'

'In Europe anyway,' he agreed. 'The ancients used to call it the Queen of the Aegean. They thought it was especially blessed by Helios, the sun god—that's why they built the statue to him.' He started the car again and drove slowly down to a large car-park on the outskirts of the town and left it in the shade of a gnarled olive tree.

'We have to walk from here,' he told her. 'The streets of the town are too narrow to take a car.'

They found a taverna and went through a bead curtain into an interior so dim that Lori could hardly see after the bright sunlight and stumbled a little. Lewis immediately took her elbow, but then let it go when she stiffened and moved away. A beaming patron led them through the back of the building into a little courtyard where bougainvillaea hung from the walls in swathes heavy with scented blossom, and in one corner water spouted from a lion's head into a stone trough a thousand years old. They sat at a table in the shadow cast by the wall, Lori taking care to move her chair so that she didn't come in contact with Lewis; the way he had treated her the previous night was still raw in her mind and now that they were alone together she felt nervous and on edge.

The menu was all in Greek, but Lewis seemed to know what it meant and had no difficulty in ordering.

'Do you like Greek food?' he asked her.

'I haven't tried very much,' she confessed. 'The food at the hotel is very unexciting, just ordinary dishes, and when I've eaten out the only thing I understand on the menu is moussaka.'

'Then I'll order for you.' He said something to the waiter who hurried away to return with glasses of ouzo as an aperitif. Lewis added water and then swirled his glass, looking down at it thoughtfully while Lori waited with some trepidation. Then he looked at her directly and said slowly, 'I'm afraid I owe you an apology.' He paused for a moment but when she didn't speak, went on, 'Last night I jumped to what seemed to be a very obvious conclusion, especially when Dean said the fight was over a girl. It was only when I talked to him this morning that I discovered the truth. I said some very harsh things to you yesterday; I'm sorry.'

It was Lori's turn to look down at her glass; she supposed she ought to say it was all right, it didn't matter. But it did matter; his accusations had hurt.

She stayed silent for so long that he said questioningly, 'Lori?'

Slowly she raised her head and looked at him. His grey eyes were regarding her intently. With difficulty she said, 'Last night I told you that you'd been wrong about me from the beginning. I pleaded with you to believe me, but you wouldn't.'

'And now you're asking me to believe that because I was wrong last night....'

'No!' Lori cut in swiftly. 'I'm not asking anything more from you—not now or ever again. I've tried to justify myself to you too many times already, but you've always chosen to believe the worst of me.' She shook her head helplessly. 'And I don't know why! You have only hearsay and gossip to hold against me, but rumours always fly around about every unknown who lands a good part, it's just a way of expressing professional envy and jealousy. Surely you know that? Okay, so in my case it was aggravated by Tony Rodgers because he was annoyed that I wouldn't have an affair with him, but....'

'Is that true? He was never your lover?'

Lori's mouth tightened. 'No. And before you ask I'll tell you that I didn't get this part by making myself available on some casting couch either,' she added angrily.

He looked at her broodingly, his eyes shadowed, while Lori watched him in hopeful expectancy. He must believe her this time, he must! It was suddenly what she wanted more than anything else in the world, that he should think well of her, though why she didn't even begin to understand.

His mouth broke into a slow smile. 'Then I'd better wish you a very belated welcome to *The Siege*, hadn't I?' and he raised his glass to clink it against hers and then drink a silent toast.

Lori sat back, still hardly able to believe that she had convinced him at last, her eyes wide with wonderment and tentative happiness, but then they were interrupted by the waiter bringing their first course.

'What is it?' Lori asked.

Lewis shook his head. 'Try it first and see if you like it.'

She looked at him rather suspiciously and gingerly tried what looked like meat in a white sauce. 'Mm, it's delicious,' she decided, taking another mouthful. 'It's chicken done in a special sauce, isn't it?'

Lewis's mouth twisted in amusement. 'No, it's not. As a matter of fact it's baby octopus.' And he laughed aloud at the expression on her face.

Lori smiled back at him. 'I've never seen you laugh before.' It was said almost on a note of wistfulness.

Instantly his face sobered. 'Have I been such an ogre to you, little one?'

Calling her that confused her a little and she answered haltingly, 'It's just that you seemed so determined to dislike me. At times you seemed quite inhuman.'

A flicker of amusement came into his eyes. 'Oh, I assure you I'm entirely human.'

'Yes, I ... I suppose you are.' In the middle of the sentence recollection of the way he had reacted in an extremely human fashion to her accusation the night before flooded back to her and flushed her cheeks to a vivid pink.

It was evident that Lewis knew exactly what she was thinking because the look of amusement deepened, but he merely said, 'Eat your octopus.'

Lori blinked and then burst out laughing. 'That is the most ridiculous expression I've ever heard!' And Lewis, too, joined in her amusement.

After that the day changed completely; the tenseness that had always existed between them just melted away and they were able to be at ease with one another, to talk and discuss the film as friends and colleagues. Lewis seemed as if he was trying to make up for all the misconceptions and odium that had gone before and he put himself out to make her laugh, telling her anecdotes about his previous films and some of the hazards he had had to contend with, and drawing her out to talk about herself. And Lori found that she enjoyed talking to him, loved making him laugh as she animatedly told him of a disastrous play she had been in in rep. where part of the scenery had fallen down, and the way he watched her, an amused lift to the corner of his mouth, made her feel good.

After lunch they left the shade of the taverna and emerged into the solid heat of the afternoon sun. She had no hat, so Lewis insisted on stopping at a tiny shop to buy her a pretty straw one.

'Haven't you learnt to wear a hat here yet?' he remonstrated as he set it on her head. 'I don't want my romantic lead going down with sunstroke. One invalid is enough,' which remark was a little dampening at first, but when she saw the smile that went with it, it didn't matter in the least. Lori had waited a long time for one of those smiles and was basking in them now. When Lewis Brent decided to change his opinion about someone he really did it in a big way!

The path up through the town to the castle was steep, but near the bottom a line of mules were tethered and several boys came crowding round, offering the services of themselves and their animals.

Lewis spoke to them and then turned to grin at her. 'It seems there are several hundred very steep steps up to the castle, but if you like you can go up on a mule. They'll even take your photograph as a souvenir of the ride for a few drachmas extra.'

Lori laughed. 'I'd love to try it—but in this dress?' She indicated her slim-line skirt.

'You could always hitch it up,' Lewis suggested.

'With all these men around? No, thanks, I'd rather walk.'

'Well, maybe we can fix something else.' He turned to one of the boys and they brought up another mule, a big animal almost the size of a horse. Lewis climbed easily into the saddle and led the animal to a mounting block. 'Come and ride side-saddle in front of me,' he offered. 'That way you won't fall off.'

Gingerly she did so, settling herself as comfortably as she could on the hard saddle and feeling his arms close securely around her.

'Okay?'

'Okay.' She raised her head to answer him and found her face only a few inches away from his. A finger of nervous excitement ran through her and again she remembered the bruising passion of his lips on hers. Hastily she looked away, laughing to try to cover her sudden tension.

'Then smile for the cameraman. Or shouldn't I tell you to do that on our day off?'

And Lori looked at him again to find him smiling down at her. So neither of them posed for the camera, after all.

The path might have been steep, but the mule-track was hardly less so, and Lori clung to the saddle but still had to lean her weight against Lewis as the animal made its way along a well-worn track through a small plantation of lemon trees, interspersed here and there with irregular patches of planted land, seemingly scratched out of the earth without any uniform size or shape. It was a far cry from the green fields of England, but Lori drank in the scenery as they made their way slowly up the hillside, her body leaning against Lewis's and his arms strong about her. She turned to make some laughing remark to him just as the mule stumbled a little and she was thrown hard against him. Immediately his grip on her tightened as he steadied her and the words she had been about to say died in her throat as their eyes met and held for a moment that seemed to last as long as time itself. All emotions, all feelings seemed to stand still—and then the moment was past as the mule-boy called out to Lewis and pointed down at another bay that had appeared below them.

'What did he say?' Lori asked rather breathlessly.

'Mm?' For a second Lewis, too, didn't seem exactly with it. 'Oh, he said I should go and have a look at that bay later, alone. He said all the tourists go there to sunbathe in the nude.' He stood up in the stirrups to have a better look and then grinned as he caught Lori's surprised glance. 'It's all right; that's the bay we're going to use for the scene where you're washed ashore and Dean finds you. I was just checking to see if a road went down to it.'

'Of course,' Lori agreed demurely. 'Why else would you want to look at it?'

He laughed again, a full masculine laugh of enjoyment and punched her playfully on the jaw. 'If I wasn't on this mule, young lady....'

Lori's eyes sparkled mischievously up into his; she felt suddenly glad to be here, glad to be alive on such a beautiful day and in such a beautiful place. It was one of those moments of pure happiness in her life which she wanted to go on for ever, but which she could only try to take in and hold in her memory as best she could; the wonderful scenery, the heat of the sun, the sound of the mule clip-clopping its slow way through heavily-scented lemon trees—and the feel of Lewis's hard chest against her shoulder, his strong arms holding her safe.

CHAPTER SIX

THEY 'did' Lindos thoroughly, from the ruins of the temple of Athene on the ancient Acropolis which stood on the edge of a sheer cliff that dropped nearly four hundred feet down to the rock-strewn sea, to the later castle built by the Knights of St John and used by them as an outpost. Lewis pointed out how they would use just the best preserved aspects for the sets and she began to understand a little of all the preparation that went into the making of a film before the actors even arrived to play in it. It was obvious that he loved his work, talking of it intelligently and well, and giving her even more insight into the depth of feeling he had for this particular film as he told her of his first visit here on a sailing holiday and the fascination he had felt when he saw Rhodes and learnt about the men who had fought and died for it.

It was late afternoon before they left the rock on which the castle still stood sentinel and made their way back down to the town. By tacit consent they chose the steps this time and found that the mule-boys had far exaggerated their number and they were also less steep than they expected. At both sides of the steps, wherever there was a bank of a convenient height, the peasant women had spread their home-made wares to sell to the tourists. Here again were the brightly-coloured rugs, but most prevalent of all were tablecloths and table-mats that the women crocheted from fine silk thread, many of them working on yet more cloths as they sat beside the dusty steps and tried to catch the tourists' attention. Lori couldn't resist a set of table-mats to take home as a gift for her mother and Lewis conducted the sale for her in Greek, so that the black-shawled peasant woman smilingly gave her some doilies as well.

She was so pleased with her purchase that she didn't look where she was going and would have tripped if Lewis hadn't caught her by the waist to steady her. Turning to thank him, Lori was slightly taken aback to see that he was looking at her with a rather strange expression in his eyes. But then it was quickly masked as he let her go and turned to walk on down the last of the steps and enter the narrow, cobbled street into the town. They found the photograph taken of them on the mule waiting for them at the bottom and Lewis immediately bought it and gave it to her with some light comment about not to dare to show it to anyone in the crew or his reputation would be ruined, but although he still talked with her, he seemed somehow to have withdrawn within himself, to have lost the free and easy manner he had shown earlier. At first Lori wondered uneasily if she had offended in some way, but then decided that he was probably thinking about the film. Not very flattering, but entirely in character.

On the way back Lewis suggested they stop for a drink and pulled up in a small village where they sat at a table outside the local taverna among the Greek men who seemed to be there at all times of the day, sitting in the shade and talking politics. Just as men did the world over, Lori thought wryly, only they seemed to have far more time to do it here on this placid island.

She refused Lewis's offer of ouzo and settled for an orange juice, pressed from oranges taken from a tree alongside the taverna. Lewis seemed disinclined to talk, looking down at his glass rather broodingly, twisting it around as if he was trying to make up his mind about something, so Lori sat back, content to watch the village coming to life again after the afternoon siesta: the shops opening one by one, the children coming out to play, the women doing their shopping. Glancing up, she found Lewis watching her, a speculative look in his grey eyes.

Immediately he set down his glass and looked away, then said abruptly, 'Lori, I want to ask you to do something for me—for me and for the film, that is.'

He hesitated, and Lori said uncertainly, 'I will, if I can, of course. What is it you want me to do?'

He picked up his glass again, swirling the white liquid in it, not looking at her. 'I want you to look after Dean for me—keep him out of trouble.'

Lori gazed at him wordlessly, a feeling of cold disappointment running through her. She realised that he was waiting for some response and tried to gather her wits. 'How do you mean—keep him out of trouble? If the other people he goes around with can't stop him from drinking too much, then I'm sure I couldn't either.'

Lewis sat forward earnestly. 'But I think you could. I think it's an act that he feels obliged to put on more than anything. Don't forget, he was completely unknown until he took part in that American serial and then he became famous almost overnight, everybody wanted him and he was suddenly a hot property. It's an image he feels he has to live up to—and yet he still wants to be one of the boys. So he tries to be friendly with everyone and overdoes it. And he thinks he can keep up with hardened members of the crew who can drink a bottle of whisky almost before breakfast and think nothing of it.' He paused, searching her face, then said with emphasis, 'But I'm sure that if the two of you went out alone together he wouldn't feel the need to act the star, he could just be himself, especially if you let him know that you didn't see anything particularly clever in having to drink to get your kicks. I'm sure it would work, Lori.'

'Are you? I'm not.' The disappointment was still there, deeper now; it had been such a happy day, but somehow it was spoilt and she wished fervently that Lewis hadn't asked this of her.

'Why not? You like Dean, don't you?'

'Yes, of course I do. But what makes you think he

would listen to me? Or even want to go out with me alone anyway, if it comes to that? He likes going out in a crowd.'

'And maybe he wants very much to go out with you but has been too nervous to ask,' Lewis said deliberately.

Lori's head came up in surprise. 'He told you that?'

His grey eyes regarded her steadily. 'Not in so many words, no. But it's quite obvious that he thinks a lot of you.'

She shrugged her shoulders in a negative gesture. 'It certainly hasn't been obvious to me. I like Dean, but that's as far as it goes. And I don't want to get involved.'

'Who's asking you to get involved? I simply want to try to keep Dean out of trouble, and I think you're the one person who can do it.'

A flash of indignation lit her green eyes. 'When I first came here you told me to keep away from the men in the crew.'

Lewis sat back and looked at her, his expression unreadable. 'So I did. But that was when I'd been given the wrong impression about you. Now I'm showing you how much I believe you by entrusting Dean to your care. He needs a woman to give him back his confidence in himself, show him that he doesn't need drink or the admiration of a crowd to maintain his image. The only way he has to prove himself is in his work.'

Lori shook her head, still unwilling to do as he asked. 'I couldn't handle him if he got drunk.'

The reply came promptly. 'Then don't let him get drunk. If he shows signs of wanting to drink too much then develop a migraine or something and make him bring you home. I'm sure you have enough ingenuity to be able to take care of that problem, but if you do get stuck, you can always phone me and I'll come to the rescue.'

She gave a small, unhappy smile. 'Just like the U.S. Cavalry!'

His mouth twisted in amusement. 'More like the Knights of Rhodes.' He leaned forward and his hand covered hers as it lay on the table. 'Will you do it, Lori?'

Her hand quivered beneath his and then she said jerkily, 'All right, I'll try, but I don't guarantee that it will work.'

His hand tightened on hers and the smile he gave her was almost warm enough to dispel the disappointment. 'Thanks, Lori. I'm sure it will. You're just what he needs.'

Lori sat in the car going back to Rhodes and pondered that last remark. I may be what Dean needs, but what about my needs? she thought rather belligerently, and then was disconcerted to find that she didn't know what her needs were. Before today she had been quite sure that all she wanted was to be on good and friendly terms with Lewis and everyone else in the crew, to have her name cleared and to know that people weren't making disparaging remarks about her behind her back. Well, now she had that, didn't she? Lewis believed her and everyone else would follow his example. So why did his proving his belief in her by asking her to help Dean leave her with this strange, inexplicable hollowness inside her? The more she pondered the question the more confused she became, and it was with a distinctly flat feeling that she said goodnight to him outside the hotel and watched him drive away to check on a set that was being put up for tomorrow's filming.

It was only after she had given her reluctant agreement to the scheme that she wondered how she was going to implement it; she certainly wasn't going to go and ask Dean outright to take her out. But as it turned out it was much easier than she expected; the stars of the film had been invited to a reception at the Governor's residence, but at the last minute Lewis decided that the time was right to do some night shooting and only she and Dean, who was now completely recovered, were able to go. That Lewis had arranged this deliberately Lori was quite certain, and she was worried that it would be obvious to Dean as well, but he seemed completely unsuspicious as he escorted her to the party, looking extremely handsome in his white tuxedo.

Dressed up as they were, they made a stunning-looking couple, drawing everyone's attention, and being the centre of an admiring crowd all evening, so both of them were ready enough to leave when the time came.

Dean sat back in the rear of the chauffeur-driven company car and gave a sigh of relief. 'Phew, I'm glad that's over! Let's stop at the nearest taverna and have a drink.'

'I've got a better idea,' Lori answered lightly. 'Let's ditch the car and walk back along the beach.'

'Are you kidding? In these clothes?'

'You can take your shoes off, can't you? Come on, don't be so stuffy.'

'Me? Stuffy?' he exclaimed indignantly, then leaned forward to tell the driver to stop as soon as they reached the coast.

The beach was more or less deserted; all the sunloungers collected into stacks and covered with tarpaulins, the thatched shades standing like rows of open umbrellas, only a few hardy people taking a midnight swim or stroll before turning in. At first they talked of

the things they had in common, but gradually Lori
drew Dean out to talk about himself. She learnt that he
had been on the fringe of acting for a long time and
then had landed a good part that really looked as if it
would lead somewhere, but the show had been a flop
and he was worse off than before with the stigma of a
bad show on his record and a girl-friend who had jilted
him because of it. Then had come the serial and with
it instant fame, but his earlier failure had left him vulnerable, he wanted to seize the fame with both hands
and yet was in constant fear of losing it again. Once
started it seemed as if he couldn't stop talking, as if
he'd been bottling it all up for a long time. And Lori
sensed that he was only truly happy when he was working because he could cope with that easily, knew exactly
where he was, it was in his private life that he was tense
and strained, not knowing how to handle his newly-
won stardom, seeking friends yet at the same time afraid
that people only wanted him because he was famous.

They stayed out very late that night, sitting on the
terrace of the hotel in the dark, in a corner sheltered
from the breeze. Lori let Dean talk himself out, just saying an odd word of encouragement here and there. As
she listened, it came to her that Lewis must have already known or guessed at most of this. He must have
seen that Dean was heading towards some kind of
crack-up, either continual drunkenness or a nervous
breakdown, both probably, and worried about what he
could do to prevent it without it becoming common
knowledge. Her respect for Lewis increased; as the
director it was his job to look after the actors and keep
them happy, but she had no idea he had so much insight. Then she gave an inward laugh of self-mockery;

if Lewis had so much insight why was it he had been so hopelessly wrong about her?

At length Dean came to an end and they sat in silence for a while until he said remorsefully, 'I'm sorry, you should have stopped me way back. I'd no right to beat my life story into your eardrums all night.'

Impulsively Lori put out a hand and touched his. 'I'm glad you told me; that's what friends are for. And you don't have to worry, it won't go any further.' She smiled at him in the moonlight. 'But fair's fair, now you'll have to listen to my life story,' she said teasingly.

Dean laughed. 'Okay, that's a promise. How about tomorrow night?'

'All right, tomorrow. But now I'm going to bed while I can still move out of this chair.'

And so began a friendship that came to mean a lot to them both, with neither of them making any demands on the other; they never even kissed other than in a friendly way. Although no one but themselves knew how platonic it was, the whole of the crew, as soon as they got wind of it, watched them carefully to see if there was any electricity generated between them in their off-screen encounters, the thought of the love scene they would have to play together uppermost in everybody's minds but their own. And that their friendship pleased Lewis it was clear; his eyes would settle on her and give a smile of approval, knowing that she had succeeded in keeping Dean away from his drinking companions. Lori was happy now that she had offered to help and glad that she had managed to hit it off with Dean and that Lewis was pleased with her. She found that she wanted the director's approbation and was continually looking for his quick smile of approval when she had played a scene well, or the glint of amusement in his grey eyes when she made some remark that made him laugh.

The next couple of weeks were among the happiest in her life; the sun seemed to fill her heart and she sparkled with youth and zest for living. The film was going to schedule and the crew working as a well-knit team, there was no more antagonism towards her and she was on friendly terms with everyone—everyone except Tony Rodgers, that was. The spiteful lies he had told about her had gained him no credit in anyone's eyes and now, when he tried to repeat or enlarge on them, he was told in no uncertain terms to shut up. Tony being Tony, this only increased his resentment against Lori even further, and so it was with a great deal of satisfaction that he shattered her present happiness.

He came over to her one morning when she was sitting alone in the courtyard outside the palace of the Grand Master, going over her lines once more before a rather important scene. 'How's the poor man's answer to Jane Fonda this morning?' he asked sarcastically.

'What do you want, Tony?' Lori asked coldly.

He sat down in Dean's vacant chair, his eyes stripping her. 'What makes you think I want anything?' he answered, the way he said it making it a definite insult.

Lori didn't answer, refusing to give him the opening he so obviously wanted, until in exasperation he said, 'I merely wondered how you were making out with your opposite number—the Golden Boy of the motion picture industry himself, Dean Farrow. Tell me, have you slept with him yet?'

'That's none of your business,' Lori retorted shortly.

'Oh, but it is. It's everyone's business. A film's success

always depends to a large extent on how hot the sex scenes are.' He paused to lend emphasis to his next sentence. 'But then I expect Lewis explained all that to you when he told you to have an affair with Dean.'

The colour slowly drained from Lori's cheeks and she stammered, 'What—what did you say?'

The look of satisfaction on Tony's face deepened and he smiled derisively. 'Why, I really believe he didn't tell you at all. How incredibly devious of our noble director! But then he has got a great deal of money tied up in this film one way and another.'

'Will you please say what you came to say?' Lori got out, her throat feeling tight and restricted.

Maliciously Tony took his time, getting the most out of it. 'It's common knowledge in the film world that a director—any director—likes to have emotional involvement between his romantic lead stars, that way when they play the love scenes the screen really sizzles. And everyone knows what a stickler for authenticity Lewis Brent is—he cares so much for this film that he'll probably have the two of you making love right there in front of the cameras!'

Forcing herself to look at him steadily, Lori, her voice cold as ice, said, 'You're completely wrong; Dean and I are just friends, nothing more. Not that I expect you to believe that, your mind's so foul you'd believe the worst of anyone. Well, now you've stirred up the dirt why don't you go back and crawl down the hole you came from?'

Realising that he would get no more satisfaction out of her, Tony gave her a venomous look and took himself off.

Numbly Lori raised her head and watched a lizard climbing the wall of the palace, he would run a few

steps and then stay very still, as if afraid that someone
might have seen him move and attack him. Not that
he had much to fear so high above the ground and
blending in with the wall so well as he did; the birds
were his only predators. For a long while Lori watched
him, her lines forgotten. She tried to tell herself that
Tony was just making the whole thing up, that Lewis's
motive in asking her to go out with Dean had been
purely altruistic with nothing but Dean's good in mind,
but the seed had been sown and the nagging doubt
stayed in her mind, making her feel wretched and uncertain.

She went to the skull session for the big scene and sat
next to Dean and opposite to where Lewis sat near his
blackboard with the camera and actors' movements all
drawn up on it. He started talking to the technical
people first as he usually did, but soon stood up to in-
dicate something on the blackboard. He always did
this, too full of restless energy to stay sitting down for
long. Dean leant back in his chair and put a casual arm
along the back of Lori's, his hand lightly touching her
shoulder. Lori felt the warmth of his hand. She looked
up at Lewis—and then knew with a suddenness that
sent her senses reeling just why the thought of Lewis
deliberately pushing her into a love affair with Dean
had appalled her so much. Other thoughts came in a
tumbling chaos and left her breathless: the way she'd
warmed to the approval in Lewis's eyes when she'd
pleased him, the tension she felt whenever he touched
her, and most of all the hurt she had known when he
had misjudged her. These and a hundred others
jumbled through her mind. She was in love with the
man and hadn't even realised it!

'Lori?'

She came back to earth and realised that they were all looking at her expectantly. She blinked and looked round at them rather dazedly, trying to gather her wits.

'Are you all right? You look pale.' Lewis was looking at her, his eyes frowning in concern.

'Yes, I—I'm fine—really. It's just...' she sought desperately for something to say that wouldn't give her away. 'It's just that it's my first big scene and I think I've got stage fright.'

They all burst out laughing, and Lewis shook his head at her, his eyes amused, but there was warmth there too. 'Halfway through the film and the girl develops stage fright! And I thought I'd heard everything!' But he took her to one side after the skull session and took pains to go through the scene carefully with her so that she knew everything she had to do. 'Just remember what I've told you and you'll be okay,' he encouraged her.

Lori nodded, but her eyes were on his face, studying each feature as if with new eyes: the firm mouth and the strong line of his jaw, the grey eyes that were regarding her under slightly puzzled brows. Had he really intended her to have an affair with Dean? Had he? She put out a hand to touch his sleeve and said tentatively, 'Lewis?' but then bit her lip and looked away. 'No, it's nothing.'

'You're sure? If you have any questions about the scene....'

'No.' She managed to smile. 'It wasn't anything important.'

He nodded and stood up. 'Okay, then let's get to work.'

The scene was to be shot in two parts: the first where Dean, as Sir Richard, still thinks she is a boy and is angry with himself and with her for his growing feelings for her, and comes home to his lodging one night—ironically—having had too much to drink, and knocks her down when she goes to help him. The second part would show his remorse and his clumsy attempts to try to help her staunch the blood flowing from a cut on her face, the break in the middle to give the make-up department time to apply the necessary wound and blood.

Just before they were about to begin Lewis came over to her. 'How's the butterflies? All gone now?'

Lori managed to smile and speak confidently. 'Of course. It was only for a moment.'

'Good.' His voice softened. 'That's my girl!'

She gazed after him in pleased astonishment as he walked back to his position by the cameras, hardly able to believe her ears. It was the nearest he had ever come to showing any feeling for her and right now it gave her the most wonderful boost to her morale just when she needed it the most. He must have cared something for her to say it, and if he did—a surge of happiness welled through her veins—if he did then he could have had no ulterior motive when he asked her to help Dean. He had said he wasn't asking her to get involved and he had meant it.

Lori played the first part of the scene better than anything she had ever played in her life; she *was* the girl, and she felt every emotion the girl would have felt; the longing to disclose her true identity and feelings and the fear that if she did the Knight would send her away and she would never see him again. And Dean too, perhaps reacting to some spark in her, played the scene brilliantly, so that when it was over and Lewis had called 'Cut!' there was a silence among the crew and then an unprecedented ripple of admiration and applause.

Still flushed with success and the heady emotions she had discovered within herself, Lori went into the house near the set and sat down in a chair to let the make-up man make her suitably gory. Lydia Grey, the wardrobe mistress, stood nearby, waiting to dirty her costume and make sure she was dishevelled enough.

'That was a great scene,' the older woman complimented her. 'You've really taken to film-making.'

Lori smiled her thanks, unable to speak for the moment as the make-up man stuck an imitation cut on her cheek, but while he went off to mix up some blood the two women chatted together, a friendly acquaintance having grown up between them over the weeks of constant costume fittings.

It was curiosity more than anything else that prompted Lori to ask, 'You know everything there is to know about films, Lydia; do directors normally have a financial interest in the films they're making?'

The woman gave a slight shrug. 'Little-known men often only get their salaries, but someone of Lewis Brent's fame, someone who can pick and choose what films he makes, is almost bound to be on a percentage of the box-office takings. Why do you ask?'

'Oh, it was just that I heard someone mention that Lewis had a lot of money tied up in *The Siege*.'

'Well, I suppose he has. Not only did he write the original story but he also formed a company, in partnership with the producer, especially to make this film. He had to get financial backing from one of the major international companies as well, of course—no small company could possibly have done it alone. And I suppose if it was a flop he would stand to lose a great deal of money, he might even be bankrupt.'

'I see,' Lori murmured rather hollowly. 'No wonder he goes to such lengths to make sure it will be a success.'

'Yes,' Lydia agreed. 'I shouldn't think there's much he wouldn't do.'

But there's one thing he wouldn't stoop to, Lori thought determinedly. She was sure of that. But it would be nice to have it confirmed by someone else. She glanced at Lydia and said casually, 'I have heard of some directors who try to encourage their romantic leads to fall for one another, just so that the love scenes come across more realistically. Does that really happen?'

Lydia raised her eyebrows. 'Of course it does—all the time. And Lewis Brent is no exception; he's done it before and he's doing it now. Why else do you think he's thrown you and Dean together so much?' She looked at Lori in astonishment. 'Good heavens, don't tell me you didn't realise that that was what he was conniving at? The whole crew's been having bets on the outcome ever since shooting started. And it's worked, too, hasn't it? You've really hit it off with Dean, if the amount of times you've been out with him is anything to go by. Most of the men bet that Lewis would get what he wanted—he usually does, some way or other.' She chuckled. 'And now all the men on the crew are fighting to get the best places when you do the love scene; they're expecting something really torrid, especially after the way you acted with Dean today.'

Then she must have seen the expression on Lori's face because her voice softened. 'Oh, don't look like that. It isn't the end of the world because everyone knows you're having an affair with Dean.'

'I'm not!' Lori interrupted forcefully. 'We're just good friends.'

Lydia grinned. 'Now where have I heard that before? All right.' She held up her hands as Lori opened her mouth to protest. 'So maybe you haven't got as far as having sex with him yet, but it's bound to happen eventually.' She laughed again. 'You're going to have to go to bed with him in the love scene anyway. So how realistic you make it depends on you—although it wouldn't surprise me if Lewis didn't persuade you and Dean to do it together in reality beforehand— just for the sake of the film, of course.'

Lydia turned away as the make-up man came back, and there was no time for anything further as they mussed her up and got her ready for shooting. Everyone was in position and waiting for her as she went to take her place on the set with Dean.

She found that she couldn't look at Lewis, but he followed her on to the set and smiled at them. 'That last scene was the best you've done in the whole film. I'm proud of you both.' He reached out to put a hand on each of their shoulders. 'You two certainly seem to have some sort of chemistry going for you, the sparks really flew in that scene. Keep that up and we're really going to have a hit on our hands!'

Lori listened to him with a sick feeling in her stomach. Of all the low-down, hypocritical...! She shrugged away from his hand, unable to bear to have him touch her. How could she have been so naïve, so childish as to believe him? And what was far worse, how could she have been so stupid as to fall in love with him? Miserably she went to take up her position on the floor and let the make-up man apply more imitation blood.

The second part of the scene was an utter mess; Lori had lost all her former brilliance and her acting was wooden and automatic, she fluffed her lines and forgot her moves, so that they had to take it time and time again. Everyone was very patient with her, but the sun was high in the sky now, the stone walls of the room in which they were working retaining the heat and adding to that of the lights over their heads. The weight and thickness of the chest flattener made her droop and she began to perspire freely under the wig.

After the ninth take the make-up man came yet again to blot her forehead and repowder it. Irritably Lori jerked away from him. 'Leave me alone, can't you? I'm sick of having my face clogged up with that stuff!' she snapped.

'I'm only trying to do my job,' he answered defensively.

Immediately Lori was contrite. 'I'm sorry. I know you are. I'm—I'm just rather hot, that's all.'

Lewis must have heard the exchange, because instead of going ahead with another take he called out, 'All right, everyone, we'll take an early lunch-break today.'

There was a general murmur of approval as the crew made for the refreshment wagon, but Lori bit her lip and turned away, ashamed that she had let her emotions interfere with her professionalism. She was sitting on the low bed which was part of the set and now Dean crossed to sit beside her.

'You okay, honey?' He put an arm round her and squeezed her shoulder.

Yesterday Lori would have taken the gesture in the friendly way it was meant, but today she couldn't help looking on it as the crew probably would—as the possessive touch of a lover. Abruptly she stood up and crossed to the Coke machine to get herself a drink. 'Yes, of course I'm all right,' she answered sharply. 'Why shouldn't I be?'

He didn't answer and she stood with her back turned towards him as she drank, willing him to go away and leave her alone, and after a moment she heard him move off the set, his armoured costume chinking as he walked. When she was sure that he was out of sight, Lori gave up all pretence of drinking and set down the monocup, her shoulders dropping dejectedly.

'Lori?'

The sound of her name when she thought that she was alone startled her and she turned quickly round to find Lewis standing at the corner of the set, watching her intently. For a moment she stared at him, her face vulnerable, but then she hastily turned away.

'It's all right, you don't have to say it,' she said tartly. 'I know I made a mess of that last scene. I know I let Dean and everybody else down and you don't have time to waste on temperamental actresses who can't get it right. You don't have to tell me, I've heard it all before!'

She expected him to make some sarcastic comment at her outburst, would almost have welcomed his anger, but he merely said mildly, 'Why don't we take a walk on the ramparts? There's a breeze from the sea up there.'

'No, thanks,' she answered shortly.

'Why not?'

'I must go over my lines and moves again. And besides, it wouldn't make any difference, I'd still boil out in the sun with this wig on.'

'Then take it off.'

'I can't, it takes too long to fix and the hairdresser would be annoyed if she had it all to do again,' Lori said defensively.

'Then she'll have to be annoyed with me, because I'm telling you to take it off,' Lewis retorted, his voice becoming sharper. He looked at her expectantly, but when she didn't move gave an impatient exclamation and reached out to pluck the wig from her head.

Lori felt her hair tumble about her face and automatically put up an unsteady hand to straighten it. Jerkily, in a last-ditch effort not to be alone with him, she said, 'It isn't only the wig. I have to wear this bodice thing, and I can't get it off myself.'

'Let me see,' he commanded.

Reluctantly Lori lifted up her tunic and showed him the bodice, strapped up tightly at the sides to flatten her chest.

'Good God!' Lewis ejaculated. 'Have you been wearing that contraption all through filming?'

'You wanted authenticity, remember?' Lori retorted caustically.

'Lift your arms up, I'll take it off for you.'

Lewis began to undo the straps, but she tried to pull away. 'No, I haven't got anything on underneath. Oh!' Hastily she pulled down the front of the tunic as Lewis undid the last buckle and pulled it off.

But he was looking down at the bodice and his voice sounded angry as he said, 'The wretched thing is soaked with perspiration—it's a wonder you didn't pass out wearing it in this heat. The wardrobe department will have to find something lighter to use, and I'll have air-conditioning rigged up on the set.' He dropped the bodice on a chair and looked at her. 'But right now we're going to take that walk.'

He led the way and Lori had no choice but to follow, but she would have given anything not to be alone with him now, not when her emotions were such a seething cauldron of love and resentment. He didn't take her to the section of the ramparts that they were using for filming, but on towards one of the unrestored towers that looked out over the sea.

'This part of the battlements up to the next tower was always defended by the English-speaking knights,' he told her. 'It was a tradition that each tongue always defended the same part of the city through all the time they were here.'

He went on casually talking, but Lori took little notice. Her fists were clenched at her sides and her heart was beating painfully because she was so close to him. She had only to reach out and she could touch him. She found that she wanted very much to touch him. As soon as they reached the tower she hastily moved away from him and went to look out to sea. There were a few boats making for the harbour, but there was little or no beach here and there were very few people about, only an old man fishing from the rocks and some small children paddling in the shallows. Lori closed her eyes and let the breeze ruffle her hair.

'Don't you think you ought to tell me about it?' Lewis's voice shattered her fragile peace and she turned slowly to face him. Immediately the sun burnt through the thin material of her tunic.

'About what?'

'About why you went to pieces when we tried to

shoot the second scene this morning,' he answered drily.

She shrugged. 'There's nothing to tell. It was just the heat—that, and not having learnt the scene properly, I suppose.'

His eyes narrowed. 'I admit the set was hot, but no hotter than yesterday and the day before; and you always do your homework, you know how that scene goes as well as I do.' He shook his head. 'No, something happened between filming that made you fall apart, and I want to know what it was.'

'I tell you it was just the heat. I'm hungry, I'm going for my lunch.'

She went to hurry past him, but he caught her arm and swung her round to face him, his voice sharp. 'Oh, no, you don't! Not until I know why....'

Lori wrenched her arm away and glared at him. 'Don't touch me! Don't you dare touch me!'

His grey eyes stared into hers. 'So I'm the culprit, am I?' he said softly. 'And just what am I supposed to have done that's upset you?'

Discretion and her temper flew away with the breeze as Lori burst out furiously, 'You've lied to me, that's what you've done! Deceived me into thinking that we were—were friends, when all the time you just wanted to use me!'

Lewis's face tightened. 'And just how am I supposed to have lied to you and deceived you?' he asked grimly.

'By telling me that you just wanted me to help Dean, when all the time you were throwing us together in the hope that we would have a love affair.'

Coldly he said, 'And just how would you and Dean having an affair benefit me?'

'By making the love scenes in the film more passionate, more authentic, of course.' Lori's voice became heavy with contempt. 'And that's all you care about, isn't it—authenticity? You don't care how you use and manipulate people just so long as you get the effect you want on the screen. You know, you're on the wrong side of the cameras. You should have been an actor. That scene in Lindos where you pretended to believe me and played on my sympathy to help Dean— why, it was masterly. You should at least have received an Oscar for it!'

'Will you listen to me....' Lewis began harshly, but Lori refused to be interrupted.

'No, I won't listen. You can do some listening yourself for a change,' she retorted. 'Dean and I are friends, nothing more, and that's how it's going to stay. All the people in the crew who've made bets on our going to bed together will just have to lose their money, and you'll know that your precious film is just that much less perfect than the way you planned it. Well, that's just too bad. You'll just have to make it less obvious to everyone the next time you lie and cheat to get what you want!' She came to an end, her voice unsteady, her eyes bright with anger in her pale face.

Lewis was glaring at her, his mouth set in a tight line. 'Who told you this?'

Lori shrugged and went to turn away. 'What does it matter?'

He caught her shoulder and pushed her roughly back against the battlements, the metal armlet she was wearing clanging sharply against the stone. 'Someone accuses me of lying and trickery and you expect it not to matter? You're going to tell me who told you even if I have to shake it out of you.'

His eyes blazed down at her and Lori instinctively

flattened herself against the wall, but she still said jeeringly, 'Why, so that you can fire whoever it was because they ruined your plans? That's just what I'd expect from you.'

'Why, you little....' He took a menacing step towards her and then stopped abruptly, his expression completely changing. 'Lori, keep still. Perfectly still.' He began to slowly reach down to the ground, but his eyes were fixed to a point near her elbow.

Lori gazed at him in bewildered astonishment. She began to turn to see what was holding his attention, but he said fiercely, 'Don't move!'

But it was too late, Lori had already caught a movement out of the corner of her eye and had seen the snake that, alarmed by the noise of her bracelet, had uncurled itself from its hole and was slithering across the wall towards her bare arm! She stood transfixed, unable to move now even if she had wanted to, and stared in fascinated horror as the snake, the green V-pattern on its head leaving her in no doubt that it was an adder, moved nearer.

Then Lewis made a sudden swift movement and knocked the creature from the wall with a piece of rock he had picked up from the ground. Lori heard the sound of the rock being brought down hard twice but had already turned away, her face in her hands, her body shaking with shock and revulsion, her breath catching on gasps of fear. Blindly she turned and groped for the steps leading from the tower, her one thought to get away in case there might be more, but then Lewis came up and took hold of her by the shoulders.

'It's all right, Lori, the snake's dead. It's all over,' he said reassuringly.

She turned to him, fear driving all other thoughts out of her mind, and clung to him unashamedly, some primitive instinct making her move close to him for protection.

'Oh God, I can't stand snakes! A boy chased me with one once when I was a child and I've been terrified of them ever since,' she stammered.

Lewis put one arm round her and with the other he gently stroked her hair until her shaking eased a little. Slowly Lori raised her head and looked at him. They were still standing very close and their faces were only inches apart as their eyes met. Lewis's hand stilled, he gazed at her for a moment that seemed to go on for ever and then lowered his head to seek her lips.

It was completely unlike the first time he had kissed her; then he had been wild and angry, but now his mouth was gentle, exploring, his hands coming up to cup her face as the kiss became deeper and her lips parted under his. She was as transfixed now by desire as she had been by fear and she made no attempt to break away from him, instead letting her arms creep round his neck and returning his kiss ardently.

At last Lewis let his hands drop to her shoulders again and he put her from him, his breathing unsteady.

'This is crazy,' he said thickly.

Lori bit her lip and looked down at the ground with eyes gone suddenly bleak.

'No, don't turn away.' Lewis cupped her chin and made her lift her head. 'I only meant that—well, that you're making me break every rule I ever made. I always swore that I'd never get involved with an actress, especially one playing in one of my own films. But now....' He lifted a finger to gently trace the outline of her cheek, the curve of her mouth.

Lori looked up at him, her eyes misty. 'Are we—involved?' she asked tremulously.

His eyes crinkled with amusement. 'Well, it certainly looks as if we're heading that way.' And he bent to kiss her again.

This time it was Lori who broke away, her cheeks flushed, her body quivering from the waves of sensuality his caresses had awakened in her. He held her close against him and she could hear his heart hammering in his chest.

Raggedly he said, 'Lori, you have to believe me; I had no ulterior motive in asking you to date Dean. I truly thought you were the only person who was in a position to help him. Darling, say you believe me!'

The endearment, coupled with the look of earnest entreaty in his eyes, convinced her that he was speaking the truth far more than any lengthy explanation would have done. Tentatively she reached up to touch his face, but he caught her hand and turned it to kiss her palm. He looked at her questioningly. 'Lori?'

'Of course I believe you. Otherwise you wouldn't have—have done this.'

'Kissed you, do you mean?'

'Yes.' And then, because it wasn't in her nature to be coy, she said impulsively, 'Oh, Lewis, I've been wanting you to kiss me again for ages.'

And so he did, with mounting passion, moulding her body against his, letting her know that he wanted her, and it was a long time before he let her go.

Then he ran a hand through his hair and said unevenly, 'We'd better get back to the set before they send someone to look for us. This just isn't the place for this kind of thing.' He helped her down the steps but then pulled her roughly to him. 'Oh, Lori, Lori! You're so lovely.' And he kissed her again. Afterwards he gave a hollow groan. 'The worst part of it is that there isn't going to be much time for us to be alone together from now on. Some special effects I wanted haven't arrived from England yet and it's put us behind schedule, so I'm afraid I'll be working till late every night.'

'But there are Sundays. We'll be able to meet then, won't we?'

Lewis shook his head regretfully. 'I'm afraid I shall have to ask everyone to work seven days a week until we finish filming, so we won't even have that. But I'll make it up to you, my darling, I promise.'

Lori tried not to let her disappointment show—and she soon threw it off. This time her scene with Dean went perfectly, and when she looked at Lewis afterwards she knew that the smile and the look he gave her were special, just for her. What did it matter if they had little time together now? At least she would see him every day on the set, and when the film was finished...? But that was too heady and wonderful, too much in the region of dreams, to even contemplate. It was enough that he had shown her that he cared, for the rest she was content to wait.

CHAPTER SEVEN

LEWIS had said that he would have to ask everyone to work harder, and he pushed himself most of all, working from early morning until late at night, a punishing schedule that left him with no free time at all. Occasionally he was able to meet Lori when he left the production office after having seen the latest rushes and worked out exactly what he wanted done the next day. But by then it was very late and he was tired, so she didn't try to keep him with her. They would just walk down through the hotel gardens to the beach and there, in a block of shadow, he would kiss her and murmur endearments that made her heart sing with happiness.

But she kept these meetings brief for another reason too; she knew that Lewis wanted her, and he was capable of rousing her sexually so much that she was afraid that if he asked her to sleep with him she wouldn't be able to resist. And she didn't want it to be like that, when they were both tired and had to work the next day. If they were going to make love, then she wanted the first time to be something very special, far away from the hotel where anyone in the crew might see them, somewhere where they could spend the evening together first and have the whole night and the next morning too, if they wanted it. Lori had no qualms about giving herself to him; she was sure in her heart that he was the one man she could love and she would give her body happily and gladly. If he wanted to get married that would be very, very, wonderful, but if not—then she would take what he was willing to give. She loved him so much that she felt humble and incredibly thankful that he cared for her at all.

Filming progressed, but not as well as Lewis would have liked. Because Rhodes was an island everything they needed had to be shipped in, and he and the producer faced constant hold-ups. Expenses seemed to add up at the speed of light on location and they just couldn't afford to waste any time; when the extra horses they wanted didn't arrive in time for a battle scene they switched to shots inside the Grand Master's palace, when the big star who was to play the Sultan Suleiman was unable to get to Rhodes on the arranged date they filmed parts of the siege itself, and when the Turkish boats weren't finished they hastily made up a set to use so that they could film the Knights' betrayal by one of their own comrades.

As Lori read the hastily amended call sheet each day she could well understand why Lewis had so little time, and she took great care not to make any demands of him and also not to let any of the crew suspect that there was anything between them. She wanted their relationship to be a solace to him, not a complication. And she knew that he understood and appreciated her reticence from the warmth in his eyes and the way he would gently squeeze her arm when he demonstrated how he wanted a scene played, or moved her to another position to see if he could get a better camera shot.

She still went out occasionally with Dean, but he seemed to have settled down a lot now that the film was well under way and he was used to the crew, and besides, they were both so tired that they didn't often feel like going out. It was gruelling work in that climate and no one was surprised when tempers sometimes erupted and bitter quarrels broke out among people who had worked together placidly for weeks and were usually firm friends. To try to relieve some of the tension the producer threw a big Independence Day party on July the fourth in honour of all the Americans in the crew, and it soon developed into a high-

spirited and rather drunken bout of horseplay as everyone worked off their excess energy in races and com-
petitions. Lori stayed for an hour or so, laughingly
dancing with everyone who asked her while all the
time keeping an eye open for Lewis who had telephoned her to say he would try and make it. But he
didn't come, and when the party degenerated into
throwing people into the pool and mattresses out of
the hotel windows, Lori decided it was time to leave.

The party helped for a while, but the Hollywood
star still hadn't arrived, so they had to rearrange the
schedules yet again and Lewis decided that, as one
boat had been built, they would go to Lindos and
shoot the scenes which came at the beginning of the
film where Lori was to be shipwrecked on the island.
The boat was a converted fishing vessel and had to
have room not only for the scenes to be shot but for
all the cameramen and essential technicians as well,
so the atmosphere was claustrophobic with everyone
getting in each other's way and people and equipment
crammed into every available inch of space. The heat,
too, on this, the Mediterranean side of the island
where there was no breeze, was intense and one of the
cameramen had already passed out before they even
began to actually film. Lori was lucky in that she was
in the shade inside the mock-up cabin where a battery-
operated fan had been set up, but for the first scene she
was wearing female clothes and the heavy skirts and
sleeves seemed to drag on her like lead weights.

They got through the first day's filming and everyone
was hopeful that the rest of the scenes would be finished with just one more day's shooting; no one wanted
a third day on that boat! Things went reasonably well
during the morning until they reached the point

where Lori had a long scene with the actor who played the part of a priest. They had rehearsed it and were made up and costumed, the cameras ready, the lights and microphones in position, and they were about to begin when there was a shout from on deck and the sound of a motorboat approaching.

'Oh hell! Now what?' Lewis exclaimed. 'Find out what it is, will you, Bill? All right, everybody, relax for a few minutes.'

Lori sank thankfully into a chair and watched while Lewis turned to talk to one of the technicians. She tried to look at him objectively, but she couldn't any more; each feature of his face, every characteristic gesture he made, was now a part of her. When they were separated she longed to see and be near him again, and when they were together on the set her heart filled with contentment and happiness. He felt her looking at him now and he turned his head, hesitated in what he was saying, then gave her the briefest of winks before turning back to finish his conversation.

Lori felt herself blushing and hastily looked down in case anyone saw her, and when she had composed herself enough to look up again she found that Bill had come back and had drawn Lewis aside and was talking to him earnestly. Lewis frowned and then they both went on deck together. They were gone for a long time while everyone sat around impatiently, smoking and talking in a desultory way. After about ten minutes Bill came into the cabin again and to Lori's surprise crossed over to her.

'Lewis wants you on deck,' he told her baldly, his tone and his face full of some inner knowledge.

She looked at him in some puzzlement but obediently went out on to the sweltering deck. Lewis was

standing alone above where the motorboat was still
tied up at the side with its driver waiting at the wheel.
Lori smiled and hurried up to him, but then faltered
as she saw the grim, set look on his face.

'What—what is it?' she stammered.

His eyes, when he loked at her, had lost all their
previous warmth, now they were as cold as winter ice.
His tone, too, froze her as he said, 'It seems that your
lover got so frustrated without you that he just couldn't
keep away any longer, so he's flown here especially to
see you. But he's a busy man on a tight schedule, so
it's only a flying visit. There's a car waiting on the
shore to take you back to your hotel now. You'd better
not keep him waiting,' he added, his voice sharp with
irony. 'If you perform well in bed he'll probably get
you another film part—just the way he got you this
one!'

Lori stared at him in horror, unable to even think
coherently under this barrage. Gropingly she said, 'Are
you—are you trying to tell me that Nicholas Hayman
is here—in Rhodes?'

'Who else has the power to tear you off the set just
as we're about to film, and order you into his bed? Or
do you have other men on your string who're likely to
turn up and demand your services?' he asked, his voice
burning like vitriol. 'I'd just like to know so that we
can rearrange the shooting schedule to fit round your
more important and lucrative activities.'

Her face very white under her tan, Lori said desperately, 'Lewis, please don't be like this. I can explain;
Nicholas Hayman isn't my lover, he's my....'

But he refused to listen, interrupting her harshly.
'My God, and to think I fell for that act of wide-eyed
innocence you gave me! What did you hope to gain by

it? Another useful contact you could use to get into more films? Is that all I meant to you? And did you really think that I was so besotted that I'd turn a blind eye to your other lovers?' His hands suddenly came up and gripped her arms, digging into her flesh so that she winced with pain. 'Well, I've news for you, you little slut. I don't share my women—and I don't handle soiled goods!'

He let her go suddenly, almost pushing her away from him so that she stumbled against the deck rail. 'Well, what are you waiting for?' he demanded savagely. 'If you satisfy him quickly enough we just might be able to salvage something of today's schedule.'

'Oh, Lewis, please—please! You've got to believe me.' Lori tried to get through his anger, but she was too choked up to speak coherently, too confused and battered to find the words she needed. She reached out to touch him in desperate appeal, but he knocked her hand from his arm contemptuously, as if it was something dirty.

She became very still then, her eyes wide and wet with tears as she stared into his stony face for a long moment, then she turned and began to climb over the rail and down into the motorboat. Her heavy skirts made her clumsy, but Lewis didn't move to help her. He turned away immediately and went back down to the cabin.

During the boat trip to shore and through all the long drive back to Rhodes Lori sat numbly, her brain unable to function, her mind filled with the searing contemptuous jibes he had thrown at her. But worst of all was the wound that cut deepest, the knowledge that Lewis really cared so little for her that he wouldn't trust her or even listen to her. The bright dream was gone, blasted out of existence as if it had never been, and she felt an overwhelming sense of loss that was worse than anything she had ever known.

She didn't cry during the journey, she was too much in a state of shock for that, and it was only when they arrived at the hotel that it occurred to her to wonder why her godfather had flown out to see her. She found him in the lobby, an open briefcase by his side as he read some papers, but he stood up and came forward as soon as he saw her. He kissed her on the forehead and held her by the shoulders while he looked at her.

'You look tired. They're not working you too hard, are they?'

'It's just the heat and this heavy costume,' Lori replied stiltedly. 'Why are you here, Uncle Nick?'

He frowned. 'Let's go to your room where we can talk.' Gathering up his papers, he thrust them haphazardly into his briefcase, an action quite unlike him as he was usually extremely tidy.

Lori looked at him with growing apprehension. 'Is it Mother? Has something happened to her?' she asked sharply.

For answer he merely took hold of her arm and led her to the desk where he asked for her key, and didn't speak again until they were in her room, the door shut behind them.

He led her to a chair and then said bluntly, 'There's no easy way to tell you: your mother is in hospital and she's to have an operation on her heart tomorrow. It's a major operation, of course, but one that is performed quite often now, and there's every chance that it will be successful and we'll have her up and about again in no time.'

For a moment the room seemed to sway and dip

like a roller-coaster and Lori had to grip the arms of the chair tightly to stop herself from fainting.

'But I—but I don't understand. Has she had a heart attack? Is that why they're going to operate?'

Nicholas Hayman shook his head. 'No, but she's been feeling unwell for quite some time and her doctor diagnosed a heart condition.' He hesitated. 'That's why she asked me to send you away for a while. She had to undergo various tests and treatments that unfortunately didn't do any good, and she didn't want you to be worried by it all.'

'What do you mean—send me away?' Lori asked in a small, tight voice.

'She asked me if I could find you a job away, preferably abroad, for a few months. I'd almost got you a part in a company that was touring Australia, but then this film part came up instead.'

Hardly recognising the strangled voice as her own, Lori said, 'So you did get me this part, after all?'

Uncle Nick looked uncomfortable. 'I admit I had quite a hand in it, but they wouldn't have agreed to take you if you hadn't been good enough.' And then, at the look on her face, he added hastily, 'I know I promised never to interfere with your career, Lori, but I didn't do this for you—I did it for your mother.'

She seemed to sag within herself, as if her spine, like her pride, had been broken. Blindly she got up and went to lift down her suitcase and started dropping clothes into it anyhow.

'What are you doing?' he asked.

'Packing, of course. What time is the next plane?'

'Lori.' He came and put his hands on her shoulders to turn her round to face him. 'Listen to me. I didn't come here to take you back with me. Your mother

doesn't even know I'm here. I—I'm afraid I broke a
promise to her that I wouldn't tell you until the operation was all over. But I thought that you had the
right to know, just in case—well, just in case.' He
dropped his hands and turned away, his voice thick
with emotion, for he was very fond of her mother.

'But I must go back to England,' Lori exclaimed.
'My mother's all I have and I want to be with her!'
All she had now, yes, and her heart grew tight at the
thought that she might lose her, too.

He shook his head. 'What good would it do? We're
powerless to help her. And right now she's being very
brave; she's made up her mind that she's going to get
well and she's being very courageous—almost cheerful
about it all. But how do you think it will affect her if
you go rushing to her bedside as if she was at death's
door? Your mother's a very sensitive woman; no matter
how you tried to hide it she'd know that you were
frightened and anxious for her. And that would under-
mine her confidence completely. She's kept you out of
this because she can't take the additional burden of
having you upset and worried.'

Lori gazed at him helplessly. 'But she's my mother. I
must go to her!' She shook her head helplessly. 'Uncle
Nick, I can't just stay on here as if nothing has happened when Mummy might ... might....' Her voice
broke.

'Nothing's going to happen to her,' he put in forcibly. 'It's just an operation that's going to make her
well again, that's all. That's how she's looking on it
and that's how you've got to, if you're adult enough to
do it.'

He sat down with her and talked to her for a long
time until he finally convinced her that she must stay.

He made her a faithful promise that he would phone her immediately he had any news, and to send for her at once if her mother should change her mind and ask for her, and at last she reluctantly agreed to stay in Rhodes. But even when he had gone, hurrying off to the airport to catch a plane that would get to London in time for him to visit her mother that night, Lori was still in half a mind to race after him.

After he had gone, she sat for a long time, lost in a fit of deep depression and unhappiness. She felt as if she'd been rejected by the two people she loved, and it hurt unbearably. Her mother had always tended to be over-protective with her and treat her like a child, being fiercely independent and never confiding her worries or problems, and even now, when she was very ill, she had turned to Uncle Nick for the comfort and support she needed, instead of to Lori who would have given it gladly if she had been allowed to. And Lewis? Tears came suddenly and she threw herself down on the bed, her body convulsed by great, tearing sobs. Why would he never believe her, never trust her?

She gave way to her unhappiness until the sound of the phone ringing jarred through her crying and made her suddenly still. It had to be Lewis or one of his assistants wanting to know when she was coming back to finish filming. Biting her fingertips, she stared at the phone as its ring seemed to become more and more impatient. Then she suddenly came to a decision and sat up. Damn Lewis Brent and damn *The Siege!* She wasn't going back today for anyone. Let him and the crew think whatever their sordid minds cared to imagine, but not for anything could she go back there and try to act as if nothing had happened, as if her life hadn't been torn apart!

Going into the bathroom, she removed her smudged make-up and changed into a simple sundress, then grabbed up her bag and sunglasses and ran out of the hotel, in a panic in case Lewis sent someone to look for her. A taxi took her into the anonymous crowds of holidaymakers that filled Rhodes and there she hired a car and drove inland away from the tourist routes. The roads weren't too busy and she drove fast, over-steering into the bends and skidding round, overtaking the few vehicles that she came upon and leaving a cloud of dust behind her as she tore along the rough country roads, letting the thrill of danger and speed take the place of that raw, bleeding hurt.

It couldn't last, of course. She took a bend too wide and the back wheels left the road. The car lurched sickeningly and she was thrown against the door as she hit a rock. For a moment it tilted and she gasped in terror as she thought that it was going to overturn, but then it righted itself and landed on all four wheels with a heavy thud. For several seconds she couldn't believe that she was safe, gripping the wheel with hands that were wet with fear. Then she somehow managed to open the door and get out, her legs shaking so much they hardly held her. There was a flat rock nearby and she sank down on it gratefully, and it was quite a while before she was able to take herself to task and mentally berate herself for being so stupid. Killing herself wouldn't do any good; that was the coward's way out, and whatever else she was, Lori was no coward. When she at last got back in the car, she drove at a careful pace and didn't arrive back in Rhodes until after the blood-red orb of the sun had drowned in the darkness of night.

The next morning the make-up man had a longer

job than usual as he disguised the dark shadows under her eyes and put extra colour in her cheeks. Lori knew that everyone was agog to know what had happened to her yesterday, but she fended off the leading questions that one or two people were brash enough to ask and sat quietly in a corner, overtly studying her script.

But on the boat there was no getting away. Lewis was waiting when she and the other actors were ferried out to it and his eyes ran over her coldly, coming to rest on her face.

His voice heavy with irony, he said, 'Welcome aboard. Are you sure you feel up to filming today? After all, you must have had an extremely tiring time yesterday.'

Lori shot him a darkling glance and walked by without answering, but he followed her and said silkily, so that no one else could hear, 'The cost of yesterday's lost production was twenty thousand pounds. I hope your lover thinks you were worth it!'

Lori rounded on him, her eyes bright with anger in her taut face, but she merely snapped, 'Are we going to start filming or not?'

He regarded her grimly for a moment, then turned abruptly away and began to give orders to the technicians.

How Lori got through that day she never quite remembered; somehow the worry for her mother and the hurt that Lewis had inflicted seemed to cancel each other out, leaving her in a state of numb passivity. Somehow she managed to act her part to Lewis's satisfaction, but between takes she went up on deck and stood alone, staring out to sea. By doing so she knew that she aroused a hornets' nest of buzzing gossip, but she couldn't help it and didn't much care any more.

The last scene that day was where she had to be washed up on the shore and Lewis wanted a shot of her gradually coming closer for a long distance, so they dropped her in the sea quite a long way out and left her to swim in alone. After about twenty yards she began to weaken, already tired from worry and a sleepless night. The shore with all the cameras and crew still looked a very long way away, but she struggled on until the swell caught her and she swallowed water. Gasping and retching, she tried to call for help. On the shore she saw a man with air tanks on his back, who was standing by in case of just such an emergency, start to enter the water and she gave a gasp of thankfulness. But then, incredulously, she saw Lewis catch hold of his arm and deliberately pull him back.

Rage exploded in her and sent a surge of strength running through her veins. Would he really let her half-drown just to get more authenticity for his film? Sheer, unadulterated fury drove her tired limbs on until she could stagger and then crawl on to the sand that was burning to her touch. She just lay there, too exhausted to move, and nobody came to help her, until she felt a shadow fall across her and looked up, dripping with sea-water, to see Dean, in his costume, standing over her.

Lewis's voice called 'Cut!' and then she heard him say, 'All right, pick her up and dry her off—we need a few more days'. filming out of her yet,' as if after that he couldn't care less whether she lived or died!

That evening her godfather phoned to tell her that her mother had come safely through the operation, but it was too early to tell whether it would be successful. But on the next few evenings the news wasn't so encouraging; her mother had developed a reaction to the drugs she had been given and was making little progress. He still wouldn't let her fly home, again giving the reason that it would only upset her mother, and this too was bitterly disappointing. 'Write to her,' he said. 'A really happy and bright letter, and that will do her more good than anything.' And somehow she managed it, writing several pages of chatty news that she made up in her head and enclosing a gift of a charm of the replica of an eye set in gold which all the natives of Rhodes wore and were convinced was a powerful talisman that warded off evil and misfortune. Her mother's lack of progress worried Lori desperately, but fortunately the American star, Craig Denton, arrived in Rhodes and everyone was busy shooting the scenes in which he appeared, so she didn't have to try to work when she was low.

When she was first introduced to him she was rather in awe of such a well-known international actor, but he soon put her at ease with his natural charm and good manners, treating her and the other actors as equals and making them all laugh with his anecdotes about his life in the film business, which had lasted over twenty years. He was also unique in that his marriage—his only marriage—had also lasted nearly that long, but his wife had been unable to accompany him on this trip.

Lori still took her walk along the beach before turning in, needing the solitude more than ever now after the nightly phone call from Uncle Nick with the disappointing news of her mother's continuing lack of progress. It was on one of her walks that she almost bumped into Craig Denton, who had also slipped out

of the hotel at night so that he could get some exercise
without being recognised and besieged by fans clam-
ouring for his autograph.

They strolled along together, talking inconsequen-
tially, but when they passed under a lamp he stopped
and said sharply, 'Have you been crying?'

Hastily Lori put up a hand to wipe her eyes. 'No,
of course not!' Then, because it was obvious that she
had, she added, 'It's nothing, really.'

He nodded and started walking again, but added
diffidently, 'Okay, but if you feel you want to talk
about it I'll be around for a couple of weeks and maybe
I might even be able to help.'

'It's very kind of you,' Lori said gratefully, 'but you
don't want to be burdened with my worries.'

He smiled, the devastating smile that had made
millions of women fall for his celluloid image. 'It's no
problem, my shoulders are pretty broad.'

He waited for a moment, but when she didn't speak
changed the subject and let the matter drop. But the
next night they walked together again and two days
later, when the news from home was still negative and
she was almost sick with worry and desperately needed
someone in whom she could confide, Lori told him
about her mother's illness. Of her break-up with Lewis
she said nothing; that was something she had to face
alone, in the privacy of her own mind and heart.

He was very kind, trying to reassure her and quoting
several instances of similar cases he had known which
had proved successful, and which Lori latched on to
greedily, but perhaps the greatest good it did her was
to talk about it and by doing so relieve some of the
built-up tension that grew worse every day.

They turned to walk back to the hotel and Craig

said, 'As a matter of fact I have some trouble at home too. My wife is unable to have children and we've already adopted two boys and were going ahead with adopting a girl last month. But then the mother changed her mind and took the baby away. That's why I was late getting here; I was involved in a mess of legal business and my wife got very upset by it all.'

'That's terrible,' Lori said sympathetically. 'Did you get the little girl in the end?'

'No, but we hope to find another one very soon.' He put a casual arm across her shoulders as they walked up through the garden. 'Hey, is that right we're doing a scene together tomorrow?'

Lori smiled. 'Yes. I'm supposed to get captured by your army and you add me to your harem.'

He raised an eyebrow expressively. 'Is that so? One of the great things about being a star is that I get all the best-looking dames in my harems. But I don't recollect we have a love scene?'

'No, I just tell you what a vile and horrible old Sultan you are for attacking the Knights, and you get terribly angry and have me dragged away to a fate worse than death.'

'And then Lewis Brent calls cut,' he added resignedly. 'I guess they think I'm getting too old for love scenes any more. What do you think?' he asked, drawing her close and giving her a mock hug and leering at her.

Lori laughed. 'Not at all,' she reassured him, returning the hug, but mention of Lewis had brought back the hurt and they walked the rest of the way in silence. She was dreading having to face Lewis again tomorrow. Dreading having his eyes run over her so coldly, so contemptuously, and even more afraid of not being able to control her own emotions, of letting him see how much he had hurt her. Because pride, and a sense of helpless outrage, was all she had left now to carry her through the last few weeks of filming.

There was a new set for her scene with Craig Denton that had been built in a disused warehouse, although now one half of it looked like a sumptuous marquee and inside it all the props you would expect to find in the tent of Suleiman the Magnificent. Luckily, Lori didn't have to wear a wig for this scene, but she was again in a long and rather heavy dress. Lydia grumbled when she put it on because she had lost weight and it had to be taken in.

'Don't you know you shouldn't go on a diet in the middle of a film?' she remonstrated. 'Or is it that you're—upset about something?' she fished, looking at her closely.

Lori's chin came up and she managed a travesty of a smile. 'No, of course not. Why should I be?' she challenged.

Lewis looked her over as he did all the actors, making sure the costumes and make-up were exactly as he wanted. His eyes paused for a moment on her face and Lori tried to look past him impassively, hoping against hope that he would put down her paleness and the tiredness round her eyes to the make-up man's skill and not to nature. With a sigh of relief she heard him tell everyone to take their places for the first run through and she went to wait on the edge of the set.

Because Craig was such a big star and his time so precious, he had a stand-in who had taken his place while the cameras were being set up and the lights arranged, and Lewis's assistant director had gone through the scene with them both separately so that they needn't waste too much time on rehearsals. At least that was the theory. But they had hardly rehearsed for five minutes before Lewis stopped them and abruptly told her to put more spirit into it.

They tried again, but he exclaimed impatiently, 'No, no! You sound as if you're just telling off a naughty little boy. You hate this man for all the suffering he's caused to the Knights and the people in Rhodes. There's got to be venom in your voice. You've got to spit the words at him.'

Three times more they went through the scene, but still Lewis wasn't satisfied, interrupting harshly until Lori was shaking with the effort of controlling her emotions and would have given anything, anything! just to be able to go away and be alone.

Craig had been very good and tolerant, but he could see better than anyone the state she was in and he suddenly rounded on Lewis and said, 'You're pushing her too hard! Give her a break, can't you?' And he firmly put an arm round her and led Lori to some chairs at the side of the set. 'Go get her a drink,' he ordered one of the staring assistants, and the man immediately hurried off to do his bidding.

'There, how do you feel now?' he asked when she had had an ice-cold drink of water.

'Much better, thank you. I—I'm sorry. I'm not usually as bad as this,' she said apologetically.

'It's not your fault,' Craig replied. 'Lewis Brent is handling you all wrong. I don't know what's got into him, he's usually on the right wavelength with his actors. Why don't you tell him about your mother's illness?' he suggested. 'If he knew what you were going through. . . .'

'Oh, no!' Lori interrupted hastily. 'I don't want anyone to know. Promise you won't tell him—anyone. Please!'

'Okay, if that's the way you want it.' He looked at her shrewdly. 'There isn't anything between you and Lewis is there?'

Lori looked away so that she wouldn't have to meet his eyes. 'No. No, of course not.' But the way her face paled as she saw Lewis walking purposefully towards them gave the lie to her words.

'I want to talk to you,' he said abruptly. 'Come to my office.'

'Now wait a minute....'

Craig started to intervene, but Lori said hastily, 'It's all right.' She put a hand on his arm and smiled up at him. 'But thank you all the same.'

His voice glacial, Lewis said, 'When you're *quite* ready.'

Biting her lip, Lori followed him to his office, which was a caravan on a vacant piece of ground nearby. He held the door open for her and she preceded him inside, then turned like an animal at bay to face him. But the attack, when it came, was completely unexpected.

For a moment he stared at her, tight-lipped, then he said grimly, 'I've got to hand it to you, nothing puts you down. Lose one lover and within days you're making it with another!'

Lori stared at him. 'I—I don't know what you mean?' she stammered.

He laughed, a harsh, unmirthful sound. 'Yes, I've got to admire you, you never give up. You're even still trying that look of wide-eyed innocence with me when you know I've seen right through you.'

Stiffly Lori said, 'Would you please say what you've got to say so that I can go?'

'All right. I've no wish to prolong this interview any more than you have.' He paused, then added deliberately, 'I just want you to know that I'm not going to let you get away with seducing Craig Denton. He's happily married and I'm going to make sure he's still that way when he leaves here!'

Lori's mouth opened in stupefaction. 'Are you—are you crazy?' she gasped. 'Why on earth should I want to—to seduce him, as you call it?'

'Because I'm not the only one who's seen through you. Nicholas Hayman must have as well and flew out here to tell you it was all over between you.'

'That isn't true!'

'No?' he answered tauntingly. 'Why else would you have been so upset that you locked yourself in your room all day and wouldn't answer the phone? And you lost me, so now you're trying to get your claws into Craig Denton.'

'That isn't true!' Lori repeated, aghast.

'I saw you with my own eyes,' Lewis said harshly. 'The producer and I were taking a late night drink on the balcony of my room and we saw the two of you walking up through the gardens.'

'So what of it?' Lori flared. 'We walked and talked, that's all. But I suppose even that's a crime in your eyes!'

'We saw you, remember? You were all over him,' he said disgustedly.

With sinking heart Lori recalled the playful hug that Craig had given her. She shook her head helplessly. 'But he's old enough to be my father.'

'So was Nicholas Hayman, but you didn't let that stop you. I wonder just how many marriages you've broken up,' he added acidly, but before she could answer went on, 'But this is one you're going to keep out of. Do you understand me? You keep away from Craig, because if you don't,' he threatened, 'I shall have no option but to tell him about your past.'

Lori gazed into his eyes, dark and cold as new steel, and felt rage and bitterness well up like a great fountain inside her. 'I hate you,' she said fiercely. 'God, how I hate you!'

His jaw tightened. 'That suits me just fine. Now, you're going to get out there and you're going to play that scene the way it should be played, and then we're going to shoot the rest of your scenes just as soon as I can arrange it so that you can get the hell out of this film!'

Later that day, Lori sat alone in the lobby of the hotel waiting for her call from England when Lewis walked through the entrance with a briefcase under his arm and carrying several cans of processed film. He paused when he saw her and then walked over to her table.

Looking down at her enigmatically, he said, 'After our little talk you played the scene opposite Craig brilliantly. I could almost have believed you really hated him.'

'It was easy,' Lori replied balefully. 'I just pretended it was you.'

He smiled thinly and raised his left eyebrow quizzically. 'Really? Then I wonder who you're going to pretend you're with in the love scene!'

CHAPTER EIGHT

As it happened, however, Lewis was unable to get rid of her as quickly as he wanted. He had to shoot the rest of the scenes with Craig Denton and then his Turkish ships were finished at last and he concentrated almost entirely on the battle scenes for over a week. Lori took advantage of this to go to the producer to ask if she could fly home for a few days on compassionate grounds, without naming them. The poor man looked uncomfortable and said he would let her know, evidently wanting to consult Lewis first, but after a short while phoned to say that she could go, but she was to leave a phone number where she could be contacted in England so that she could fly back immediately they needed her. Within an hour Lori was packed and heading for the airport and the first available plane to London.

During the last few days her mother had been given a new drug and was at last responding to treatment, so Uncle Nick raised no objection when Lori phoned him and told him that she was going straight to see her. Even if he had it wouldn't have made any difference; there was a quiet determination in her manner now and she wasn't to be put off any longer.

After the first few shocked and emotional moments on seeing her mother looking so pale and thin, Lori talked to her brightly and encouragingly, not letting her see past the cheerful mask to the unhappiness beyond. She visited twice a day, during which time the older woman improved remarkably, recovering all the lost ground, and the doctors were so pleased with her that they spoke of letting her go home before too long.

The rest of the time Lori spent alone, taking long walks beside the Thames and slowly coming to terms with herself. It was a relief to get away from the close-knit community of the film crew, away from the hotel where she always felt as if she was living in a goldfish bowl, but most of all to get away from Lewis. The pain was still there, a real, physical pain, every time she thought of him, but gradually over those few days she built a wall, solid as those of mediaeval Rhodes, about herself. She became far more self-contained, but lost some of the sparkle and impetuosity of youth in the process. All I've done is grow up, she told herself, and wondered wryly if an unhappy love affair was an essential part of that process.

Perhaps her mother sensed the change in her, perhaps it was only the recent acknowledgement of her own mortality, but by the time Lori returned to Rhodes there was a far better understanding between them and they parted on better terms than they had been for years, as adult equals rather than mother and daughter.

When Lori arrived back on the island it was almost as if she had never been away; everyone was still working seven days a week in a desperate attempt to finish on schedule, there were the usual problems of last-minute changes in the shooting script, lack of supplies from England, and trouble with the locals. The sun was hotter than ever in the cloudless sky, drying the earth to dust and spreading a layer of greyness over the vivid green polish of the hibiscus leaves and the brilliant crimson of its flowers; only in the hotel gardens which were watered every day were the plants and lawns still the bright green of spring.

The next morning, at the location site, the first person she met was Dean. He greeted her warmly, giving her a hug, and telling her he was glad to see her.

'How's the film progressing?' she asked him.

He groaned and raised his eyes heavenwards in mock agony. 'I tell you, Lori, you were real lucky to get away. Lewis has been working us worse than any slavedriver. I've hardly been out of this tin can for two weeks,' he told her, indicating his armour. 'And look,' he walked away from her in a rolling, wide-legged gait. 'You see this? I've been in the saddle for so many days on end that I can't even walk straight any more. But at least today will probably see the end of the scenes with all the local extras who've been playing soldiers of one side or the other.'

'You've finished all the battle scenes?'

Dean nodded. 'Yeah. Today we're shooting the Knights leaving the town and sailing away from Rhodes, which will come at the very end of the film. There's still quite a bit of shooting to do, but Lewis wants to pay the extras off as soon as possible.' He nodded his head in a pointing gesture. 'Talk of the devil! Come on, we'd better go and let Lewis give our costumes the once-over. Although why he wants to see mine again when he must be as sick of it as I am, I'll never know. You know what?' he went on. 'The day I take this darn thing off for the last time I'm going to pour a can of gasoline over it and set light to it, or perhaps I might....'

He continued in the same vein, but Lori wasn't really listening. She followed him with the other actors to line up in front of Lewis as he looked carefully over each person, although at this late stage in the film the wardrobe department had become so efficient that he had few criticisms to make. As he walked slowly along Lori had time to observe him, if not dispassionately, at least without any visible show of emotion. He looked drawn and very tired, his face thinner than she remembered, and for a few wayward seconds she felt her heart contract and an overwhelming surge of love, of wanting to hold and comfort him, well up inside her. But it was as quickly and determinedly fought down and the face she turned to him when he reached her was completely remote and impassive.

He stopped in front of her and she saw his jaw tighten. His eyes ran over the long, dark gold gown she was wearing and he gave a curt nod, whether of greeting or approval she didn't know, perhaps both. Then he moved on down the line.

At the skull session shortly after, he said in his usual crisp and businesslike manner, 'For Lori's benefit I'll explain that we're undecided on the romantic ending of the film and are going to shoot two different versions. In both you go apart from the general exodus of the Knights from the city and go to a boat with an English flag, obviously on your way back to England. You stand and watch the Knights leave. In one version, Sir Richard, having previously rejected you because of his chastity vows, stays with the other Knights and embarks with them. In the second version he leaves them and joins you. We'll have to see how the rest of the film works before we decide which version we'll use.'

Lori's part was easy; she had nothing to say and had only to stand on the gangplank of the ship and watch and wait. It was very early in the morning, the dawn only just breaking behind the ancient walls of the city, now made to look battle-scarred and breached, as the great gates near the harbour slowly opened and the first of what was left of the once glorious company of Knights filed out of their home. The actor who played the Grand Master headed the procession, a grey-haired, venerable old man who still managed to sit his horse with dignity in face of his humiliation and sadness, and behind him came the last of his brave men, many of them wounded and carried on stretchers by their servants, and all the townspeople who had chosen to go into exile with them.

Lori knew it was only a film, had seen all the actors having their 'wounds' applied, had only to turn her head to see the cameras being backed away from the head of the procession, but even so it moved her and tears came into her eyes as she realised that it must have looked very, very much like this in reality. Trust Lewis for that; he would make sure that every detail was just as authentic as he could make it.

They managed to finish both versions that day and everyone heaved an audible sigh of relief. Working with local extras, especially the large number that was needed for a film such as this, and particularly with those that spoke a different language from the crew, was always a difficult and trying time, but now everybody felt as if they had surmounted a huge obstacle and the end was in sight at last.

During the next few days Lori worked on small, unimportant scenes with the assistant director and didn't see Lewis at all, but after filming one day the assistant called after her and said, 'Oh, I nearly forgot, Lewis said to tell you that we'll be filming the love scene tomorrow and you're to call in at Wardrobe before you go home.'

Lori nodded her acknowledgement. 'I'll go along there now.'

She found Lydia Grey in the midst of packing discarded costumes into huge trunks. 'Just getting some of this stuff ready to ship back to England,' she explained. 'Lord, I hope I get assigned to some nice present-day film next time, where everyone wears jeans and sweaters.'

Lori smiled slightly. 'In that case you'll probably get some way-out sci-fi movie like *Star Wars*.'

Lydia made a piteous face. 'Oh no, don't wish that on me, for heaven's sake!' She looked at the younger girl pensively. 'I heard you went back to England. Not bad news or anything, was it?'

Immediately a shutter came down over Lori's eyes. 'No, I just decided to take advantage of the shooting schedule and have a break. The assistant director said you wanted me for a costume fitting,' she said pointedly, changing the subject.

'All right,' Lydia said good-humouredly, 'I can read the "Keep Out" sign.' She shook her head. 'No, not for a costume fitting. I want to know whether you wear a bikini top when you sunbathe.'

Lori looked at her in astonishment. 'Yes, of course I do. Why on earth do you want to know?'

'So that I can get the make-up department to give me some stain to put on your white bits tomorrow. Nice little mediaeval girls didn't have bikini marks on their boobs,' she explained with a grin.

Her voice suddenly tight, Lori said stiltedly, 'Are you saying that I'm supposed to appear nude in the love scene?'

'Not completely nude, only your top half.' Lydia frowned. 'Although I believe you were to be bare at first, but Lewis changed his mind and said just your breasts would do.'

'Did he?' Anger broke the surface like boiling surf. 'How very big of him! Well, you can tell Mr Lord Almighty Brent that I have no intention of baring any part of my anatomy for his rotten film, and if he doesn't like it then he can just fire me and shoot the whole damn thing all over again!' And she strode out of the room, slamming the door viciously behind her and leaving Lydia gaping at her with her mouth wide open.

As had become her habit since her return from England, Lori had dinner sent up to her room, but she hardly picked at the food before pushing it away, and when the next day's call sheet was pushed under her door she didn't even bother to go and pick it up. Angrily she paced up and down the floor, seething with resentment. How dared he take for granted that she would willingly expose her body to Dean, to the crew, and eventually to the millions of people who would see the film? The thought of thousands of leering, faceless men staring at her image, revolted her, but even worse would be having to meet men who had seen the film, knowing when they looked at her just what they were imagining. The thought of it made her flush with embarrassment and increased her determination to hold out against him.

All evening she waited for the phone to ring with a summons to Lewis's office, but as the night dragged on without anything happening she began to hope that she had won an easy victory. At eleven she began to prepare for bed and was undressed and about to take a shower when there was a peremptory knock at the door. For a moment she fought a strong impulse not to open it, but then squared her shoulders; if Lewis Brent wanted a battle then he was certainly going to get one! Tightening the knot on her towelling bathrobe, Lori opened the door.

Lewis was leaning nonchalantly against the wall, his hands in his pockets. His grey eyes ran over her briefly, but his expression was unreadable. Evenly he said, 'I'm sorry to call so late, but I got held up with the latest rushes. I rather wanted to talk to you, but as you're obviously not dressed to go down to the bar, perhaps I might come in for a moment?'

She had expected him to be blazingly angry, was ready to give as good as she got and slam the door in his face, but his calmly casual approach threw her out of top gear and before she quite realised what was happening he had walked past her and into the room, picking up the call sheet as he did so.

'Now just a minute. . . .'

But he took no notice of her indignation and strolled through into the main room.

'You don't happen to have a drink, do you? It's been rather a long day.' And he sat down heavily in the only available chair, tossing the call sheet casually aside as he did so.

Still standing holding the door, Lori looked at him suspiciously, alert for some kind of trick. But he *did* look very tired. Slowly she shut the door and walked into the room. 'There's only some wine,' she said uncertainly, indicating her dinner tray.

'That will do fine, thanks.'

She poured it for him and gave him the glass, taking care not to touch him. But he didn't seem to notice and took a long drink as if he was very thirsty. Afterwards he swirled the rest of the wine round in the glass, looking down at it broodingly, almost as if he had forgotten she was there. Then he glanced up and saw her watching him and seemed, with some difficulty, to bring himself back to the present.

'I'm sorry, things on my mind. Aren't you going to join me in a drink?'

'No, but help yourself if you want some more.' She felt awkward standing up in front of him, but the only place to sit was the bed. After a moment of indecision she perched on the edge, pulling the skirts of her robe tightly across her knees.

Lewis poured himself another glass of wine and then leant back in the chair, looking as if he would very much have liked to have closed his eyes and gone to sleep.

Despite herself she said, 'You've been working too hard.'

'Hm? Oh, it's always like this towards the end of a film when you're trying desperately not to overrun your schedule. But another week will see it finished.'

'And then you'll be able to have a holiday before you start something else?'

He gave the ghost of a smile. 'I'm afraid it doesn't work like that; there's still another three months' work to do on *The Siege* before it's ready for release. The footage has to be edited, the sound effects and the musical score put in—without them you have just a disjointed series of pictures.' He looked at her directly. 'How about you? Have you anything lined up?'

Lori shook her head. 'No, I haven't made any plans.'

He stood up, pressing his shoulders back as if his body ached. He was wearing a blue linen shirt, open at the neck, the cuffs turned back casually, and he seemed very broad and tall, his presence dominating the room. Stepping to the open windows, he looked out for a moment, then turned towards her. Here it comes at last, she thought, the tension rising within her like something tangible.

'Lydia tells me you refuse to appear topless in the love scene. Tell me, is it because of your principles or because you want to annoy me?'

Lori's features tightened and she answered coldly, 'It's a matter of principle. And there's nothing in my contract that says I have to take my clothes off!'

'No,' he agreed, but added reasonably, 'But there is a clause that states that you will follow my direction.'

'Not as far as that,' Lori rejoined icily. 'It doesn't matter what you say, I'm not going to do it.'

Exasperatedly he said, 'Then would you please tell me how the audience is supposed to know that Sir Richard has discovered you're a girl when they're not allowed to see for themselves?'

Rather unsteadily Lori answered, 'That's your problem.'

Lewis put a hand rather wearily through his hair. 'Yes, I suppose it is, although better actresses than you have taken their clothes off when the scene calls for it. But all right, I shall just have to try and think of something else.'

He fell silent, and Lori looked down at her hands clenched in her lap, hardly believing that he had given in with so little fight, and wondering what solution he would think up to the problem as he stood so silently beside her. But it seemed that he hadn't been thinking about it at all, for soon she felt his hand on her hair as he gently ran it through his fingers. Softly he said, 'I missed you, Lori.'

She turned startled eyes up to him, but before she could speak he reached down and drew her to her feet, holding her near to him.

'No!' She tried to push away from him, but he held her firmly by the arms, his face very close. 'No, Lewis, please! I don't want this.'

'But I do. Desperately.' And he locked his hand in her hair and pulled her against him, his lips seeking hers with a passionate hunger.

'No!' Frantically she struggled to get free, pushing her hands hard against his chest, but his grip was like a vice and her struggles only seemed to increase the vehemence of his embrace. Realising that it was useless she grew rigid within his arms, willing herself not to respond. But he took no notice, his lips like fires that burnt her skin as he kissed her eyes, her throat, the curve of her cheek, coming back to importune her mouth, forcing her lips apart, his passion bruising and hurting her.

And then suddenly she was lost. She could fight the desire rising in her like a great tidal wave no longer and allowed it to engulf her completely. Her body relaxed and she gave a little moan of surrender. She felt him give a gasp of triumph and then her head began to whirl as he kissed her again, holding her close, close against him. His hands began to explore, loosening the knot of her bathrobe and sliding inside. Lori's breath caught in her throat as her breasts hardened under his caressing hands, and then somehow the bathrobe had dropped to the floor and he was stooping to carry her to the bed and lay her gently down on it.

Opening her eyes, Lori reached up her arms to him. 'Oh, Lewis, Lewis, my darling!'

He stood leaning over her, his breathing uneven, his eyes dark with desire as he slowly ran them over the length of her body.

'You're very, very lovely,' he said softly. 'Perfect.' Then his eyes came back to her face as she looked up at him, still lost in the sensuality he had awoken in her. Abruptly his voice, his features changed completely and he straightened up. Coldly he said, 'And I rather think it would be a great pity if the cinemagoing public were deprived of a sight of all that perfection. So tomorrow you'll come on the set just like this and I'll have you completely naked as I intended in the first place. Why stop at your waist when you're so willing to take the rest off?'

For a moment Lori could only stare at him, too rudely awakened from desire to take in what he was saying in such a harsh, callous voice. She shook her head, trying to speak, but unable to think coherently. Then realisation hit her like a physical blow and she made a wild lunge away from him. But Lewis was too quick for her and caught her arms, pinioning her down on the bed.

'You beautiful little bitch! Did you really think I'd let you get away with it? You've taken your clothes off for me just as quickly and easily as you have for countless other men, and now you're going to do it for this film. I'm not going to let you turn the love scene into a furtive grope under a blanket, like some dirty little X picture. The cinema is an art form as much as any other and I'm not going to let you cheapen it. That scene is going to be beautiful, do you hear me, beautiful!' He stood up suddenly, letting her go. Contemptuously he added, 'And your body's right for what I want, even if you do sell it to the highest bidder.'

With hands that shook so much that she could hardly grasp it, Lori pulled the coverlet over herself and stared up at him, hair tumbled, eyes very large in her pale face. 'Get out of here, get out of my room.' Her voice was little more than a whisper. 'I—I won't do what you want.'

His eyebrows rose mockingly and there was a definite jeer in his voice as he turned at the doorway and said softly, 'Oh yes—you'll do it.' And then he was gone.

The set seemed deathly quiet as Lori walked on to it the next day. It was very dark outside the circle of lights directed on to the mock-up of Sir Richard's lodgings and her eyes were unable to penetrate the blackness beyond them. Not that she wanted to, because she knew that out there as many of the film crew who could find a reasonable excuse to do so, and many who couldn't, had packed themselves in what was supposed to be a closed set, agog with avid curiosity. And out there too was Lewis, his eyes coldly watching her. She shivered despite the heat of the arc lights and pulled the dressing gown she was wearing closer around her.

Earlier she had had to sit through the skull session with Lewis, a period in which she had contrived to look fixedly at the blackboard and not meet his eyes once. Then he had told her and Dean to go away somewhere quiet and rehearse the scene by themselves while the cameras were set up.

The rehearsal had been a dismal failure. They had both been dressed then, of course, but even so they were too embarrassed to go through the scene. And Dean was nearly as tense as she was. It was the first time he had been asked to play in a nude scene and he was as nervous and ill at ease as Lori. So in the end they gave up and sat and talked about what they would do when the film was finished and they went home.

Lori crossed over to the small truckle bed in which she was to lie when the scene started and sat with her back to the cameras while she waited to be told to start. The hairdresser did some last-minute adjustments and then Lewis called, 'All right, everybody, let's go.'

As she slipped into the bed, the hairdresser helped her off with the gown and then Lori lay back, her eyes turned towards the wall. A sharp command brought a sudden silence to the murmurings on the set and then she heard the sharp rap of the clapperboard. She was supposed to be having a nightmare and make a noise which would waken Dean who was asleep in the next room, the shot cutting from one to the other of them. That part was easy enough; she had her eyes shut and could almost pretend that she was alone, that there weren't hundreds of eyes staring at her from out of the darkness, not to speak of the two cameras only a few feet away.

She heard Dean come into the room and move over to her bed where she lay in a patch of moonlight. He was supposed to pull the blanket up around her, but as he took it up to touch the swell of her breasts and then to slowly pull the blanket down to discover the truth. She felt him do all this, but then he was supposed to caress her while she was still asleep. Her eyes were still closed but her heart was thudding in her chest as she waited. She felt his hand warm on her breast and then suddenly shuddered and turned her head away, unable to stand it any longer.

'Cut!'

A buzz of noise broke out again and Lori felt Dean give her shoulder a reassuring pat and then heard him go away again. Then Lewis's voice coming nearer, saying, 'Lori, you must remember to lie still the first time he touches you, you don't wake up until. . . .' He broke off abruptly and she knew that the hand she had hastily raised to cover her face had been too late—he had seen the silent tears coursing down her cheek.

In quite a different voice he said slowly, 'You'd better go back to the make-up department and get your face fixed again.'

Not looking at him, she tried to blink away the tears, and fortunately the hairdresser hurried forward to help her to cover herself and then she almost ran off the set. The make-up man took one look at her face and blessedly refrained from comment, just getting out his magic box to do again what he had already spent quite a long time getting right earlier.

It took all Lori's courage to get up out of the chair when he at last stepped back and said she was ready. Her legs seemed to have lost all their strength and she had to push herself up by her hands, holding tightly on to the back as she swayed unsteadily.

'Are you all right?' his voice was sharp with concern.

Lori managed to stand up straight. 'Yes, I'm—I'm fine. Really. I'm sorry you had it all to do again.'

She turned to the door just as it opened and she grabbed the back of the chair again, but it was only Lydia and her heart slowly resumed its normal beat.

The older woman looked at Lori with an uncertain frown, then said, 'Lewis told me to tell you that he's decided to shoot the scene slightly differently. He's going to fuzz it—that means shoot it slightly out of focus,' she explained. 'So he said you might as well wear this.' She held out what looked like a pile of flesh-coloured tights.

'What—what is it?'

'It's a body stocking. It covers you from neck to toe. It would show up on a close-up shot, of course, but on a fuzzed shot it doesn't make any difference.'

Her hand trembling, Lori slowly reached out and took the garment from her, looking down at it un-believingly. Then she caught a glimpse of the make-up man's worried face and managed a smile. 'It's all right, I'm not going to cry and ruin my face again.'

And immediately she had said it, she realised with cynical bitterness that the only reason Lewis could have given in to her was to avoid the possibility of that happening.

As Lori stepped out of her taxi below the road leading to the Amboise Gate she could already hear faint sounds of music carrying through the stillness of the night. Slowly she walked up between the closed souvenir stalls that lined the narrow road, across the bridge over the moat and through the archway between the squat watch towers into the old city. For a moment she paused to touch the grey stone. Strange to think that this was the last time she would ever see this mediaeval fortress that had found its way into her heart from the first moment she had seen it, spreading its mighty walls like strong arms around the town it guarded. She could come back again, of course, for a holiday some time in the future, but even as the thought crossed her mind she knew that she never would. There had been too much sadness, too much brief ecstatic happiness here for her ever to be able to bear to come back. For a moment she rested her forehead against the stone, still warm from the sun, then straightened abruptly and walked quickly towards the Grand Master's palace.

The noise of music was louder here and all the floodlights usually reserved for the Son et Lumière performance had been turned on so that the building stood out gaily in the darkness. A small crowd of people had gathered near the iron gates leading into the courtyard even though it was so late, and Lori had to push her way through to where a security man was letting in members of the film crew or guests with invitations.

He opened the gate for her and looked disapproving. 'You shouldn't have come alone, miss. I thought Dean Farrow was supposed to bring you?'

'He was,' Lori acknowledged. 'But I wasn't ready and told him to go ahead.'

No point in telling the man that she hadn't been going to come at all. That she had no heart to join in the wind-up party that the producer was throwing for the crew, various local dignitaries, and several members of the British and American Press who were in Rhodes to do stories on the making of the film, now that *The Siege* was finally finished. She had been going to spend her last night in Rhodes quietly packing and getting ready for the journey home, but she had been filled with a great restlessness, so that in the end she had changed into a black evening dress with shoestring shoulder straps, that fell in loosely swathed layers to her elegantly sandalled feet. Her hair she had swept back and added a chignon hairpiece, impulsively tucking in a blood-red hibiscus bloom picked on her way down through the hotel garden. She looked slim, sophisticated and beautiful, a picture of youth and vitality, until one looked closely and saw the haunting sadness in the depths of her green eyes, emeralds that had lost their brilliance.

The whole of the ground floor of the palace had been given over to the crew for the party and the big double doors stood wide open, ablaze with light. Almost reluctantly Lori went through them, ready even now to turn and run back to the sanctuary of the hotel, but she was late and there was no one in the ante-room leading to the main salon, so she was able to go and stand near the doorway and look in without being observed. At one side of the room three Greeks in traditional dress were singing and playing bouzouki music, and Lori smiled slightly as she saw a great many of the crew trying to emulate some Greek dancers who were demonstrating a linked-arm folk dance. The music was loud and tuneful, the people happy and laughing, having partaken liberally of the ample food and drink provided in a further room opening off the main one. Everyone was in the throes of letting their hair down, although the party was nowhere near as wild as it would become once the Rhodian visitors had left and the crew really started to drink and enjoy themselves.

Dean was in one of the dancing groups and when he caught sight of her he waved and pointed towards one of the tables at the side, indicating that he'd saved her a seat. Lori nodded and smiled, but hesitated for several minutes before deciding to stay for a while longer. She waited until the dance had ended and everyone was going back to their tables before she moved forward. But as she stepped through into the main room she suddenly found her way blocked and glanced up to find Lewis deliberately standing in front of her, a grim, angry look on his face. Catching her arm, he jerked her round and hurried her back into the empty ante-room out of sight.

'Do you mind?' Lori said indignantly. She tried to free herself, but he kept hold of her arm. 'How dare you....'

But she couldn't finish because Lewis swung her round to face him and said harshly, 'I'm not going to let you do it, do you hear me? I'm not going to let you go out there and create a scene in front of the Press and everyone else just to get your own back on your ex-lover!'

Lori stared at him in bewilderment. 'I don't know what you're talking about. Let go of me!' She tried to break free, but she might as well have tried to bend a steel bar.

Her answer only seemed to infuriate him more and he gave her an angry shake. 'Stop lying! I've seen through that innocent façade of yours, remember? You know damn well that Nicholas Hayman is here, although why the man should be fool enough to come here after he....'

Astonishment made her still and she said incredulously, 'He's here? Now?'

Sneeringly Lewis said, 'As if you didn't know!'

But Lori hardly heard him, her face had lit up at the news and she swung round eagerly towards the main salon, but Lewis pulled her back.

'You heard me. I'm not going to let you go to him.'

'Oh, don't be so ridiculous,' Lori said impatiently. 'I'm not going to have a row with him.'

'No?' He took hold of her other wrist and looked

into her face. 'My God, I don't believe you were. You were going to go in there and try to get him back, weren't you? After all he did to you! Don't you have any pride in yourself? You let a man treat you like dirt, throw you aside like a piece of rubbish, and still go running to grovel at his feet! He hurt you before, do you really think he wouldn't do the same again the minute it suited him, even if he did take you back? Do you?'

His voice had risen and he began to shake her again. Savagely he said, 'Can't you see what you're doing to yourself? Living with a man old enough to be your father. Throwing your youth and beauty away on any man who wants it!'

He shook her so hard that her teeth rattled, but with a sudden violent jerk Lori broke away from him and stood trembling, her eyes fixed on his. As angry now as he, she said fiercely, 'What does it matter to you what I do? What the hell do you care about me?'

He stared back at her, his lips twisted into a thin bitter line. 'It matters,' he said heavily. 'Because I care. God help me, you're everything I despise in a woman, and yet I still care!'

She had automatically begun to rub her bruised wrists, but now she grew very still and gazed into his face. The noise from the party seemed to fade away and she felt as if there was no one there but the two of them, facing each other in the sudden stillness.

'Lori!'

The spell was shattered as someone called her name and swinging round she saw her godfather emerge from the other room and walk quickly towards her.

'Lori, I've been looking all over for you. How are you, my dear?' Coming up to her, he put a familiar arm round her and kissed her on the cheek.

She heard Lewis make an involuntary sound and turned to see a bleak look in his eyes before he turned abruptly to leave.

'No, don't go.' Lori put out a hand and caught his sleeve. Steadily she said, 'I don't know whether you've met Nicholas Hayman?'

His face a taut mask, Lewis nodded briefly. 'I believe we met fleetingly some time ago when we were looking for sponsors for *The Siege*.'

'That's right, I remember.' Uncle Nick held out his hand, but Lewis didn't appear to see it. 'I must congratulate you on finishing the film to time, and from the early reports I've had of it, it seems certain that it will be a great success.' He turned to Lori and Lewis would have gone away, but she kept a tight hold of his sleeve. 'I've got some news that you're going to be the first to hear. I'm getting married.'

She felt Lewis give a jerk of surprise, but Lori smiled. 'Now I wonder who that could be to,' adding deliberately, 'Daddy.'

Nicholas Haymen laughed delightedly. 'Now you've spoiled my surprise! Yes, your mother's agreed to marry me at last. Just as soon as she's recovered from her operation.'

Lori let go of Lewis's sleeve and moved forward to kiss her godfather. 'I couldn't be more pleased. I know you'll both be very happy.'

For several minutes they talked together about her mother while Lewis stood silently by, but then Lewis said slowly, 'Your mother has been ill?'

'Yes.' It was Uncle Nick who answered. 'But surely you knew that when you gave Lori permission to fly home?'

'No,' he answered unevenly. 'She didn't say why she wanted to go back to England.'

Quickly Lori turned to her godfather and said, 'Uncle Nick, I think you owe Lewis an apology. He feels that I got the part in this film because of your influence and that's partly true, but I—well, I'd like him to know what really happened.' And then, without looking at Lewis, she turned and hurried out of the building, leaving the two men alone.

The courtyard was almost as well lit as the inside of the palace and Lori instinctively turned towards the iron gate that led on to the ramparts of the old city. To her relief she saw that it was open and she quickly ran up the steps, through the gate and along the top of the old walls until she was out of sight of the palace, only then slowing to a walk. The moon shone brilliantly out of a clear sky and lit the ancient buildings far more kindly than any floodlight, mellowing the ancient stone and turning it from grey to gold.

When she came to the part where Lewis had brought her once before Lori stopped and looked around. Behind her the outlines of the Turkish mosques and pantiled roofs of the houses were thrown into dark silhouette against the sky and in front the surf broke endlessly on the shore. It was very quiet, the soft sound of the waves fading into the background and no human noises reaching to break the peace and silence of the place.

She didn't know how long she stood there, gazing out to sea, but presently she heard footsteps hurrying towards her and she turned expectantly.

Lewis stopped as soon as he saw her. 'I hoped I might find you here.' He sounded out of breath as if he had been running. Slowly he climbed the steps and came nearer. 'Aren't you afraid of snakes?'

'I—I didn't even think about them.'

He stood a few paces away, looking at her intently. He seemed to be at a loss for words, to be searching for the right ones. He opened his arms in a helpless gesture. 'Lori, I....' And then suddenly he was close beside her. 'Oh, my darling, I love you so much!'

With a little sob she went into his arms, let him crush her to him as if he couldn't get close enough, as if he'd never let her go.

'Oh, Lori, I've been such a damn fool. How can you ever forgive me after the things I've said to you, the way I treated you....'

Her fingers went up to cover his lips and quieten him. 'It doesn't matter, not any more.'

But he wasn't so easily silenced. 'We could have been so happy these last weeks if I hadn't jumped to the wrong conclusions. Why didn't you tell me then that he was your godfather?'

Slowly Lori answered, 'Just because you jumped to the wrong conclusion so easily, were so quick to believe the worst of me, I suppose. If you had so little trust in me, then there didn't seen any point in—in....' Her voice broke and she turned her head away.

'Oh, my poor little love!' Lewis put a hand under her chin and gently turned her to face him. 'I've made a hell of a mess of things, haven't I? I fell in love with you the first time I saw you. I turned round to meet this cheap little actress who'd blackmailed her way into my film and it was as if I'd been kicked in the stomach. You looked so lovely, without any make-up and your hair dishevelled. My first thought was that the reports I'd heard about you must be wrong, totally wrong. But then I'm afraid cynicism took over and made me feel bitter that the one girl I'd waited for all these years should be the type I most abhor.' He paused and then said roughly, 'And I was brute enough to take that bitterness out on you.' He let go of her suddenly and thrust his hands into the pockets of his dinner jacket, staring moodily out to sea. 'Then when you, and the way you always behaved, convinced me that you were telling the truth, I was so thankful that I could scarcely believe that I'd found happiness at last, had it really within my grasp. But when Nicholas Hayman came it seemed that there could be no other explanation for his wanting to see you, especially when he refused to give one himself, and then the bitterness came back, only far worse, because I thought you'd made a fool of me.' His hands bunched into fists in his pockets. 'These last weeks have been hell, wanting you, loving you, and yet thinking all the time that you. . . .'

'Stop it!' Lori caught his arm and pulled him round to face her. 'It's over, it doesn't matter. Not now.' She reached up to put her arms round his neck and said huskily, 'Oh, Lewis, hold me. Hold me close.' He did so, burying his face in her hair, and for several minutes she stood still within the circle of his arms, just letting the sheer joy of being there engulf her. This was the hour she had waited for for so long, had wanted so badly. To feel his arms round her, his strength and warmth enfolding and protecting her, and to know that he loved her, that even when he thought her cheap he had been unable to deny his love for her.

She stirred and reached up to touch his face, gently tracing the outline of his jaw and then his lips. Softly she said, 'Lewis, there's never been anyone else. Even though, that day you came to my room.... You see, I—I loved you so much that I would have ... I thought you wanted me.' She floundered in embarrassment as she remembered, and looked away.

'Lori, are you trying to tell me—are you saying that it would have been the first time for you?' he asked incredulously.

'Yes.' Still she couldn't look at him.

'Oh, my darling girl!' It was said on a note of wonder, almost of awe. 'And you would have given yourself to me, even in those circumstances?'

Lori laughed a little. 'By then I'd lost all power to resist.'

He smiled in return and said, 'If you only knew the effort it cost me not to make love to you. You looked so lovely lying there, holding out your arms to me. And I wanted you so much that it was like wounding myself to be cruel to you. And then, when we came to shoot the love scene, it was all for nothing; when I saw you cry and realised that it really mattered to you, I suddenly knew that I couldn't bear to let the world see you as I had seen you—as I've kept seeing you and wanting you in my every waking moment ever since,' he added softly. 'And I'm afraid you're going to have to marry me very soon, my darling, because if we should even happen to find ourselves alone together for any length of time in the proximity of a large double bed, then I just won't be answerable for the consequences.'

He bent his head and began to kiss her throat, the lobe of her ear, her cheek. 'Now that I come to think of it,' he said insinuatingly, 'there's a *very* large bed in my hotel room.'

Lori gurgled with laughter and pushed him away.

'Oh, no! I want to be properly engaged first. I'll marry you as soon as you finish work on *The Siege* and not before,' she said firmly. 'So you'll just have to work hard and get it done quickly.'

'Slavedriver,' he said in mock despair. Then he smiled down at her, the look that was hers alone back in his eyes. 'Did I happen to tell you that I love you?' he asked softly.

'I believe you did mention it,' Lori replied, her voice uneven.

'Well, you'd better get used to it, because I intend to say it again—often.' And then he drew her to him and kissed her, gently at first but with a rising tide of passion that flamed like a forest fire and left them both trembling with emotion when at last they drew apart.

It was some time before they moved to leave the ramparts, but before they returned to the palace, Lori looked back along the line of the ancient walls and said wistfully, 'We will come back here, won't we?'

'Of course,' Lewis assured her. 'Just as often as we can.'

Lori turned to him with a smile. 'All my life I've waited for a knight in shining armour, but I never thought I'd have to come to their island to find one.'

He frowned a little. 'Don't put me up on any pedestal, Lori. I'm just a man who has a very interesting job, that's all.'

Seriously she answered, 'I know. I've grown up a lot since I came here. I think I was too naïve, too sheltered before.' Then she gave a smile of pure happiness. 'So instead I'll settle for a director in a dinner suit.'

Lewis grinned. 'Well, perhaps I might be able to

manage the knight as well. When I edit the film I'll let Sir Richard go with you instead of the Knights of St John.'

Lori tucked her arm into his. 'I'd like that,' she said sincerely.

They turned to walk away, and behind them the first faint rays of dawn began to spread their triumphant aubade across the sky, carrying the haunting songs of long-forgotten battle-cries and the memories of ancient glories on the breeze.

How long have you been reading

Harlequin Presents...?

Did you know that
Harlequin has been publishing
these beautiful love stories
for more than eight years?

Now... Harlequin offers you
a golden opportunity
to purchase exciting
favorites from the early
Presents' list.

Harlequin Presents
◆ *Collection* ◆

GREAT LOVE STORIES NEVER GROW OLD...

Like fine old Wedgwood, great love stories are timeless. The pleasure they bring does not decrease through the years. That's why Harlequin is proud to offer...

HARLEQUIN CLASSIC LIBRARY

Delightful old favorites from our early publishing program!

Each volume, first published more than 15 years ago, is an enchanting story of people in love. Each is beautifully bound in an exquisite Wedgwood-look cover. And all have the Harlequin magic, unchanged through the years!

Two **HARLEQUIN CLASSIC LIBRARY** volumes every month!

Available **NOW** wherever Harlequin books are sold.

Here's how to get your volume NOW!

MAIL IN	$	GET
2 SPECIAL PROOF-OF-PURCHASE SEALS*	**PLUS $1 U.S.**	**ONE BOOK**
5 SPECIAL PROOF-OF-PURCHASE SEALS*	**PLUS 50¢ U.S.**	**ONE BOOK**
8 SPECIAL PROOF-OF-PURCHASE SEALS*	**FREE**	**ONE BOOK**

*Special proof-of-purchase seal from inside back cover of all specially marked Harlequin "Let Your Imagination Fly Sweepstakes" volumes.
No other proof-of-purchase accepted.

ORDERING DETAILS:

Print your name, address, city, state or province, zip or postal code on the coupon below or a plain 3" x 5" piece of paper and together with the special proof-of-purchase seals and check or money order (no stamps or cash please) as indicated. Mail to:

**HARLEQUIN
ROMANCE TREASURY
BOOK OFFER
P.O. BOX 1399
MEDFORD, N.Y. 11763, U.S.A.**

Make check or money order payable to: Harlequin Romance Treasury Offer. Allow 3 to 4 weeks for delivery.

Special offer expires: June 30, 1981.

PLEASE PRINT

Name

Address

Apt. No.

City

State/Prov.

Zip/Postal Code

Let Your Imagination Fly Sweepstakes

Rules and Regulations:

NO PURCHASE NECESSARY

1. Enter the Let Your Imagination Fly Sweepstakes 1, 2 or 3 as often as you wish. Mail each entry form separately bearing sufficient postage. Specify the sweepstake you wish to enter on the outside of the envelope. Mail a completed entry form or, your name, address, and telephone number printed on a plain 3"x 5" piece of paper to:
HARLEQUIN LET YOUR IMAGINATION FLY SWEEPSTAKES,
P.O. BOX 1280, MEDFORD, N.Y. 11763 U.S.A.

2. Each completed entry form must be accompanied by 1 Let Your Imagination Fly proof-of-purchase seal from the back inside cover of specially marked Let Your Imagination Fly Harlequin books (or the words "Let Your Imagination Fly" printed on a plain 3" x 5" piece of paper. Specify by number the Sweepstakes you are entering on the outside of the envelope.

3. The prize structure for each sweepstake is as follows:

Sweepstake 1 - North America
Grand Prize winner's choice: a one-week trip for two to either Bermuda; Montreal, Canada; or San Francisco. 3 Grand Prizes will be awarded (min. approx. retail value $1,375. U.S. based on Chicago departure) and 4,000 First Prizes: scarves by nik nik, worth $14. U.S. each. All prizes will be awarded.

Sweepstake 2 - Caribbean
Grand Prize winner's choice: a one-week trip for two to either Nassau, Bahamas; San Juan, Puerto Rico; or St. Thomas, Virgin Islands. 3 Grand Prizes will be awarded. (Min. approx. retail value $1,650. U.S., based on Chicago departure) and 4,000 First Prizes: simulated diamond pendants by Kenneth Jay Lane, worth $15. U.S. each. All prizes will be awarded.

Sweepstake 3 - Europe
Grand Prize winner's choice: a one-week trip for two to either London, England; Frankfurt, Germany; Paris, France; or Rome, Italy. 3 Grand Prizes will be awarded. (Min. approx. retail value $2,800. U.S., based on Chicago departure) and 4,000 First Prizes: 1/2 oz. bottles of perfume, BLAZER by Anne Klein (Retail value over $30. U.S.). All prizes will be awarded.

Grand trip prizes will include coach round-trip air-fare for two persons from the nearest commercial airport serviced by Delta Air Lines to the city as designated in the prize, double occupancy accommodation at a first-class or medium hotel, depending on vacation, and $500. U.S. spending money. Departure taxes, visas, passports, ground transportation to and from airports will be the responsibility of the winners.

4. To be eligible, Sweepstakes entries must be received as follows:
Sweepstake 1 Entries received by February 28, 1981
Sweepstake 2 Entries received by April 30, 1981
Sweepstake 3 Entries received by June 30, 1981
Make sure you enter each Sweepstake separately since entries will not be carried forward from one Sweepstake to the next.

The odds of winning will be determined by the number of entries received in each of the three sweepstakes. Canadian residents, in order to win any prize, will be required to first correctly answer a time-limited skill-testing question, to be posed by telephone, at a mutually convenient time.

5. Random selections to determine Sweepstake 1, 2 or 3 winners will be conducted by Lee Krost Associates, an independent judging organization whose decisions are final. Only one prize per family, per sweepstake. Prizes are non-transferable and non-refundable and no substitutions will be allowed. Winners will be responsible for any applicable federal, state and local taxes. Trips must be taken during normal tour periods before June 30, 1982. Reservations will be on a space-available basis. Airline tickets are non-transferable, non-refundable and non-redeemable for cash.

6. The Let Your Imagination Fly Sweepstakes is open to all residents of the United States of America and Canada, (excluding the Province of Quebec) except employees and their immediate families of Harlequin Enterprises Ltd., its advertising agencies, Marketing & Promotion Group Canada Ltd. and Lee Krost Associates, Inc., the independent judging company. Winners may be required to furnish proof of eligibility. Void wherever prohibited or restricted by law. All federal, state, provincial and local laws apply.

7. For a list of trip winners, send a stamped, self-addressed envelope to:
Harlequin Trip Winners List, P.O. Box 1401, MEDFORD, N.Y. 11763 U.S.A.
Winners lists will be available after the last sweepstake has been conducted and winners determined.
NO PURCHASE NECESSARY.

Let Your Imagination Fly Sweepstakes

OFFICIAL ENTRY FORM

Please enter me in Sweepstake No. _____

Please print:

Name _____

Address _____

Apt. No. _____ City _____

State/ Prov. _____ Zip/Postal Code _____

Telephone No. area code
( )

MAIL TO:
HARLEQUIN LET YOUR
IMAGINATION FLY SWEEPSTAKE No. _____
P.O. BOX 1280,
MEDFORD, N.Y. 11763 U.S.A.
(Please specify by number, the Sweepstake you are entering.)